ESCAPE TO GOA

MEN GONE WILD

ISHAN DWIVEDI

NewDelhi • London

BLUEROSE PUBLISHERS
India | U.K.

Copyright © Mr. Ishan Dwivedi 2025

All rights reserved by author. No part of this publication may be reproduced, stored in a retrieval system or transmitted in any form or by any means, electronic, mechanical, photocopying, recording or otherwise, without the prior permission of the author. Although every precaution has been taken to verify the accuracy of the information contained herein, the publisher assumes no responsibility for any errors or omissions. No liability is assumed for damages that may result from the use of information contained within.

BlueRose Publishers takes no responsibility for any damages, losses, or liabilities that may arise from the use or misuse of the information, products, or services provided in this publication.

For permissions requests or inquiries regarding this publication, please contact:

BLUEROSE PUBLISHERS
www.BlueRoseONE.com
info@bluerosepublishers.com
+91 8882 898 898
+4407342408967

ISBN: 978-93-6783-900-3

Cover design: Yash Singhal
Typesetting: Namrata Saini

First Edition: March 2025

Preface

Life is often a blend of routine and rebellion, the mundane and the extraordinary. But every so often, the opportunity to escape the ordinary presents itself, offering a glimpse into a world of indulgence, excitement, and unrestrained freedom. This book chronicles the wild adventure of four middle-aged men—friends bound by years of shared memories and the ever-present pull of nostalgia. What starts as an innocent getaway to Goa turns into a whirlwind of chaos, temptation, and lessons learned the hard way.

At the heart of this story lies a simple truth: the desire for adventure and freedom doesn't fade with age. No matter how many responsibilities weigh down on us, the yearning for youthful exuberance lingers. The men in this story find themselves caught between the allure of their fantasies and the harsh reality of their lives, creating a thrilling and unpredictable journey.

Their trip to Goa is not only full of mistakes, impulsive decisions, and moments of joy, but also deep reflections about their lives and the relationships they've built. While they may have ventured far from their families and responsibilities, the journey leads them back to a realization that the most important connections are often the ones closest to home.

But as their wild trip ends and the dust settles, one thing is certain: the craving for adventure, for the unknown, never truly fades. And so, the seeds for their next wild escape—this time to Bangkok—are already planted.

This book isn't just about the pursuit of thrill or the recklessness of youth; it's a look at how the journey we take with friends can reveal the deepest parts of ourselves, often in the most unexpected ways. Through humor, chaos, and a fair share of mistakes, these four friends discover that while they may not be able to outrun their responsibilities, they can still chase excitement—even if it's just for a little while.

So, buckle up for a ride full of misadventure, camaraderie, and the timeless truth: men will be men. And their journey is far from over.

Enjoy the ride.
The Author

The Author

ESCAPE TO GOA

Have you ever craved a break from the monotony of life, an unapologetic escape to rediscover freedom, excitement, and connection? *Escape to Goa* is not just a story—it's an electrifying journey that unravels the human longing to break free from the chains of responsibility, if only for a fleeting moment.

Meet Ankit, Rajesh, Sandeep, and Amit—four friends bound by years of camaraderie, shared secrets, and a knack for bending the rules. Each year, these middle-aged rebels craft elaborate lies and schemes to carve out a slice of unrestrained liberty in Goa, India's vibrant coastal paradise. But what begins as an exhilarating getaway soon spirals into a whirlwind of moral dilemmas, reckless choices, and life-altering consequences.

The allure of sandy beaches, pulsating nightlife, and intoxicating freedom sets the stage for a tale that blends humor, suspense, and raw introspection. From the euphoric thrill of their arrival to the chaos of a night gone disastrously wrong, the journey is as gripping as it is unpredictable. As the friends find themselves entangled with the local police, dangerous goons, and their own fractured morals, readers are drawn into a visceral exploration of friendship, temptation, and the cost of fleeting indulgence.

At its heart, *Escape to Goa* is a story of contrasts: the unshakable bond of male friendship tested by lies and impulsive decisions; the eternal struggle between morality and the pursuit of pleasure; and the unexpected beauty of love blossoming in the unlikeliest of places. Through Amit's poignant relationship with Ananya, an escort whose presence challenges societal norms, the narrative unearths themes of redemption, vulnerability, and connection.

The vivid backdrop of Goa isn't just a setting—it's a living, breathing character that immerses readers in its magic. From sun-drenched beaches to moonlit misadventures, the sensory details transport you to this idyllic escape while leaving you questioning the fine line between adventure and disaster.

Escape to Goa isn't just for thrill-seekers or those yearning for a laugh-out-loud adventure. It's a mirror, reflecting our shared desires to escape, to break free, and to live without restraint—if only for a moment. For men grappling with middle-age monotony, for women curious about the complexities of male friendships, and for anyone who has ever questioned where the boundary lies between fun and folly, this book strikes a chord.

Prepare for an emotional rollercoaster that will keep you on the edge of your seat, cheering for the characters' victories, cringing at their missteps, and questioning your own boundaries long after you've turned the final page.

So, what are you waiting for? Pack your mental bags, leave your inhibitions behind, and let *Escape to Goa* transport you to a world of laughter, chaos, and revelations—a world where freedom and consequence dance inextricably together.

Acknowledgements

In Loving Memory of My Late Grand Parents, Mr. Ram Kumar Mishra & Mrs. Maya Mishra

This book is dedicated to the cherished memory of my late grandparents , Mr. Ram umar Mishra & Mrs. Maya Mishra, whose love, wisdom, and blessings have been my guiding light. Their unwavering support has been a constant source of inspiration throughout my life.

First and foremost, I would like to express my heartfelt gratitude to my parents, who have been my pillars of strength, love, and inspiration throughout my life. Their unwavering belief in me gave me the courage to pursue my dreams.

To my Mausi(s), who instilled in me the values of hard work and perseverance, and to my sister and brother-in-law, for their constant encouragement and support – I am forever grateful.

To my father-in-law and mother-in-law who entrusted me with their daughter without whom nothing would have been possible.

I owe a special thanks to my wife, Srishti, for being my unwavering companion in this journey. Her late-night coffee, tireless support and endless patience kept me going during the most challenging times. To my beloved children, Rudra and Rudranshi, my beloved Nephew Avi, and my cousins, your smiles and love filled me with motivation to accomplish this dream.

A heartfelt thank you to my dear friends, Ankur Mishra, Varun Kohli, and Ish Prakash Shukla, for their constant support, encouragement, and belief in me. Your confidence in my abilities has been a great source of strength.

I am deeply grateful to Mrs. Shruti Pawagi and Mrs. Medha Awasthi, for their meticulous editing, valuable suggestions, and thoughtful design work added polish and finesse to this book.

A special mention to my engineer friends from the WhatsApp group "PUBG & ALCOHOLISM," my banking group "CORE FRIENDS," and my colleagues at my bank's branch– thank you for your faith in me and for keeping the camaraderie alive, even during my busiest days.

Finally, I extend my deepest appreciation to BlueRose Publications for recognizing the potential in my work and providing me the platform to share my words with the world.

To everyone who has been a part of this journey, thank you from the bottom of my heart. This book wouldn't have been possible without your unwavering support and belief in me.

– Ishan Dwivedi

Contents

Introduction to the Four Friends 1
Chapter 1: The Reunion in Kanpur 10
Chapter 2: The Flight to Freedom 22
Chapter 3: The Arrival in Goa 24
Chapter 4: Tito's Lane and Temptation 29
Chapter 5: Svetlana and Nadya: The Deal 34
Chapter 6: The Wild Night Gone Wrong 42
Chapter 7: The Chaos 49
Chapter 8: The Aftermath 56
Chapter 9: Reflection and Regret 66
Chapter 10: Ananya's Arrival 71
Chapter 11: Four Days of Bliss 77
Chapter 12: Amit's Momentarily Spark 104
Chapter 13: Emotional Farewell 110
Chapter 14: Back to Reality 115

Introduction to the Four Friends

Once upon a time, in their college days, these four men were the epitome of youthful exuberance—charismatic, adventurous, and always the life of the party. They had it all: good looks, the confidence that comes with popularity, and the kind of charm that turned heads wherever they went. But as time passed and they entered adulthood, their lives veered into a predictable routine. Their days became consumed by work, family responsibilities, and the weight of their choices. The same men who once had the world at their feet now found themselves trudging through their 9-to-5 bank jobs, yearning for a break from the monotony, needing to feel alive again.

Here's a closer look at the four friends:

Amit – The Dreamer Trapped in the Grind

Amit was once the embodiment of charisma and ambition. In his college days, he was the heartthrob everyone admired—a magnetic presence who could captivate a room with his quick wit, charm, and intellect. Whether it was dissecting literary classics, debating philosophy, or weaving humor into casual gossip, Amit had a way of making every conversation unforgettable. He was a dreamer, an idealist who believed he could shape the world around him.

But life, with its unrelenting currents, had other plans. Now in his mid-40s, Amit's dreams lay buried beneath the weight of mortgages, rising bills, and the monotony of his job as a middle-tier manager at a bank. What once promised excitement and growth had turned into a mind-numbing routine of spreadsheets and customer queries. His marriage to Shweta, once a partnership fueled by passion and shared dreams, had become another casualty of time and stress. Their conversations had dulled, replaced by discussions of chores, children's school schedules, and what to cook for dinner.

As the years wore on, the toll of Amit's stagnant lifestyle began to show—not just emotionally, but physically. A recent doctor's visit revealed troubling news: high cholesterol and an early warning of heart disease. The man who once brimmed with vitality now felt trapped in a body weighed down by stress and neglect. Every morning, he felt the faint ache of chest tightness, a grim reminder that time was slipping through his fingers. His doctor's advice to exercise and watch his diet seemed almost laughable—when would he find the time between work and family obligations?

Despite the rut he found himself in, a small ember of longing still flickered deep within Amit's soul. He yearned for the man he used to be—the adventurous spirit who embraced life with open arms. When an unexpected opportunity for a trip to Goa came his way,

Amit found himself wondering: could this journey rekindle the fire he'd thought long extinguished?

Sandeep - The Kind-hearted Man Who Lost His Edge

Sandeep had always been the heart of everything—the kind of person whose kindness and warm-hearted nature could instantly make everyone feel at ease. With his genuine kindness and listening capability, he was everyone's go-to for lifting spirits and offering unsolicited advice.

Lately, though, his warmth felt more like a shield than a gift.

Nine years ago, Sandeep had fallen hard and fast for a woman he believed was his forever. Their love story had been nothing short of cinematic—marked by impromptu late-night drives, whispered plans for the future, and a passion that made the world seem brighter. But love has its cruel twists. By the ninth year, the woman he adored betrayed his trust, leaving him with nothing but shards of a heart that had given too much.

Still reeling from the pain, his family intervened, deciding it was time for him to move forward. That's how Shalini entered his life—his wife of six months, chosen through an arranged marriage he'd reluctantly agreed to. Shalini was everything he couldn't fault—kind, understanding, patient—but around her, Sandeep felt paralyzed by fear. Fear of opening up, fear of being hurt again, fear of trying and failing to build something real. Every conversation with her felt like navigating a minefield, his walls firmly in place to avoid vulnerability.

The once-vibrant spark that defined him now felt dimmed. Adding to this, his monotonous bank job drained whatever joy he had left. A career he'd once viewed as a path to stability now felt like an endless cycle, a cage from which he couldn't escape.

For Sandeep, Goa wasn't just a holiday destination—it was a lifeline. He craved the chance to reconnect with the carefree man he used to be, to laugh freely without the weight of cynicism, to simply feel alive again. Yet deep down, he knew the ghosts of his past and his lingering fears weren't going to be left behind so easily.

Rajesh - The Family Man with a Distant Dream

Rajesh was always the reliable one. The dependable husband, father, and friend. He had a strong sense of responsibility and took pride in being the pillar of his family. But beneath his well-constructed life, Rajesh always felts like a ghost of his former self. The adventurous, carefree man who once desired to explore the world and chasing memories, now seemed like a distant dream.

His wife, Priya, and children were his world, but somewhere along the way, the spark in his marriage began to fade. He no longer found joy in the small things; family dinners had become predictable, and the quiet evenings at home felt like an endless loop.

The bank job he'd taken for financial security had instead become a daily grind, draining the life out of him.

Despite his longing for escape, Rajesh's inherited humor remained his strong suit. He had mastered the art of hiding his frustrations behind the veil of jokes and sarcastic comments. His friends relied on him to diffuse the tense situations with quick wit, and his timing is impeccable. When Rajesh jovial self was in full swing, there was a flicker of something deeper in his eyes, a mix of nostalgia and yearning. It wasn't about jokes or remarks, it was about holding onto the pieces of himself that still believed in adventure, spontaneity, and joy of feeling alive. Goa, to Rajesh, represented a chance to rediscover the joy of living for himself again—just for a brief moment—away from the constraints of family life.

Ankit - The Silent Thinker Who Forgot to Live

Ankit was always the quiet observer, the one whose watchful eyes caught what others missed. His sharp mind could connect dots that seemed invisible to everyone else, earning him a reputation as the dependable problem-solver among his friends. Yet, despite his insight and intelligence, Ankit had spent much of his life on the sidelines, watching instead of truly living.

At 38, Ankit's life looked perfectly stable from the outside. He had a secure job at a bank, a loving wife named Neha, and two children who adored him. But beneath this calm exterior lay an unspoken restlessness. His days followed the same predictable rhythm—work, family responsibilities, and a quiet, self-imposed routine. His marriage, though steady and warm, lacked the passion and spontaneity it once had.

Neha was the backbone of their household, especially as she took on the care of Ankit's aging parents. Their declining health meant she carried a heavy daily burden, leaving her physically and emotionally exhausted. While Ankit deeply admired and respected Neha for her unwavering dedication, the weight of their shared responsibilities was creating a quiet distance between them. Their conversations had shifted from dreams and aspirations to schedules, appointments, and tasks that needed ticking off a never-ending list.

The spark that had once defined their relationship was dimming, and Ankit felt its absence acutely. On the outside, he maintained a cheerful demeanor, a facade designed to keep the family spirit alive. But inside, he grappled with a growing emptiness. He hated seeing Neha worn down by their life's demands, and yet, he hated even more how far they had drifted from the dreams they once shared.

With every passing day, Ankit found himself yearning for something more—more connection, more excitement, more freedom. His thoughts often wandered back to his younger years, a time when the world seemed full of possibilities and he hadn't yet been bound by the routines of adulthood. A chance to reclaim some of that freedom had finally arrived: a trip to Goa with his closest friends. It was an opportunity to step out of his familiar role as the quiet thinker and rediscover the version of himself that he feared he had lost.

But the trip came with its own weight. Neha wouldn't be joining him—she couldn't leave his parents in her absence, and her relentless schedule left no room for such escapes. The thought of going without her only added to Ankit's guilt. He admired Neha's selflessness, yet he couldn't shake the feeling that their life together was draining them both.

As the departure date approached, Ankit found himself caught between excitement and doubt. Could this trip help him reconnect with the man he used to be? Or would it simply serve as a fleeting distraction from the life he had resigned himself to? The answers lay somewhere on the horizon, waiting for him to take the first step.

The Escape They All Needed

Each of these men, in their own way, had become prisoners of their lives. The dreams they once had, the adventures they once sought, had been buried beneath layers of responsibility. Their marriages—while full of love—had become predictable, and their work lives were stifling. They had become versions of themselves they barely recognized—men who had once been full of life, now resigned to the mundane tasks of adulthood.

But Goa promised a different reality. It was their chance to reconnect with each other, with their youthful selves, and to rekindle the sparks of adventure that had once made them feel unstoppable. For Amit, Sandeep, Rajesh, and Ankit, it was not just about a holiday—it was about rediscovering a piece of themselves that had been lost along the way. The escape they so desperately needed was just one trip away.

The question was, could they leave behind the burdens of their responsibilities, if only for a while, and embrace the chaos and excitement of youth once again? And would they learn from it, or would they fall into the same patterns they had always known?

Their journey to Goa was about to begin, and with it, an adventure that would change everything—for better or worse.

This preface sets the stage for the story that follows, showing how these four friends—once full of promise and vigor—now find themselves yearning for an escape from their ordinary lives. Their trip to Goa is the perfect catalyst for them to face their regrets, rediscover parts of themselves, and, perhaps, make peace with the choices they've made.

CHAPTER 1

The Reunion in Kanpur

Kanpur National Bank's central branch was buzzing with its usual weekday energy. Phones rang incessantly, customers lined up impatiently, and the air-conditioning, barely holding against the summer heat, hummed feebly. The day felt long, the clock ticking slowly than usual. Maybe it was because of the endless anticipation for the Goa trip just round the corner or the looming figure yelling at us like we'd just committed a crime.

"**Fuck!** We lost another huge client!" boomed Mr. Dinesh Malhotra, the General Manager of Kanpur National Bank, his voice slicing through the stale office air like a blade.

The four middle-aged men seated before him—Amit, Ankit, Sandeep, and Rajesh—shifted uncomfortably in their seats. The walls of the modest conference room seemed to close in as Mr. Malhotra paced furiously, his polished shoes clicking against the tiled floor.

"Do you all realize what this means? Another *corporate account* gone! And this time to some godforsaken fintech startup! What the hell are you all doing here? Playing solitaire on your computers?"

Amit, the Senior Relationship Manager, adjusted his glasses and offered a placating smile. "Sir, it's not like we weren't trying. Their demands were—"

"I don't care what their demands were, Amit!" Malhotra's voice shot up a few decibels. "This is not *trying*. This is *failing*. And I don't have the patience for this anymore."

Ankit, who managed credit operations, leaned forward as if he was about to speak, but decided against it. Beside him, Sandeep sat rigid, a pen twirling deftly between his fingers. Rajesh, the Marketing Head, stared blankly at a spot on the wall behind Malhotra, his face unreadable.

Malhotra stopped pacing and faced them with a glare that could drill through steel. "Let me make this *very clear*—if we lose one more major client, you'll all find yourselves transferred to Chennai faster than you can say 'Kanpur.' I'm not kidding. Do you want to spend your midlife figuring out real estate rates in a city where you don't even understand the language?"

"No, sir," the four chimed in unison, their tones dutifully remorseful.

Malhotra dismissed them with a wave, signaling the meeting was over.

The men filed out of the conference room one by one, leaving behind the stifling tension of Malhotra's tirade. Once they were back at their desks in the open-plan office, the façade of guilt and professionalism quickly melted away.

Amit was the first to speak, dropping into his chair and swiveling lazily to face the others. "Chennai, huh? I wouldn't mind the dosas and sambhar."

Ankit snorted, loosening his tie. "Sure, and sweating through your shirt by 8 AM every day. Sounds fantastic."

"Malhotra can shove it," Sandeep muttered under his breath, tossing his pen onto his desk. "We're not the ones signing clients away to those fintech guys. What does he expect? We're bankers, not magicians."

Rajesh smirking, leaned back in his chair and folded his arms. "Honestly, I don't care if they transfer me. Less meetings, less headaches. Maybe I'll even pick up Tamil while I'm there."

The group chuckled, their voices low but tinged with a rebellious camaraderie. They were all too seasoned to take Malhotra's threats seriously. A career in banking had taught them one universal truth: nothing ever changed, no matter how loud the yelling got.

"Alright, gentlemen," Amit said, standing up and stretching. "Back to looking busy. After all, we've got those *immediate results* to deliver."

The others laughed, exchanging knowing glances as they returned to their desks, settling into their familiar routines. The General Manager could rant all he wanted, but deep down, they all knew the game: survive the day, collect the paycheck, and make just enough effort to keep the wheels turning.

Suddenly phone screen displayed a message from Rajesh on their WhatsApp group, titled *Chennai Conference*:

Ankit wrote – "What's this???"

Rajesh: Tea stall at six. Don't be late. After Malhotra's rant, our Annual Goa Escape is a must. We've got planning to do.

Ankit smirked. Rajesh had always been the overexcited one in their group, especially when it came to their annual Goa trips. Glancing around to ensure no one was watching, Ankit typed back:

Ankit: Relax, bhai. It's all set. I'll even pack my sunscreen.

At precisely 6 PM, the four friends gathered at their usual spot: a small, nondescript tea stall tucked away in a quiet corner of Civil Lines. The stall owner, Ramu, had served them for years and knew better than to ask questions about their hushed conversations.

Sandeep was the first to arrive, nervously fiddling with his phone. At 35, he was the youngest of the group and the most reluctant participant in their escapades. Having been married just six months ago, he was still in the honeymoon phase, and the thought of lying to his wife, Shalini, made him break into sweat.

Ankit arrived next, slapping Sandeep on the back. "What's with the guilt face? You look like you're about to confess to a murder," he joked.

Sandeep managed a weak smile. "Shalini keeps asking questions. What if she finds out? She's smarter than me, bhai."

"Relax," Ankit said, waving a hand dismissively. "Just keep it simple. The more you explain, the more suspicious she'll get. Say it's a last-minute conference, and you had no choice. Works every time."

Before Sandeep could respond, Rajesh arrived with his usual jovial self. At 38, he was the group's comedian, always ready with a joke or a sarcastic comment. He handed Ankit a cup of tea and sat down, grinning.

"Priya thinks I'm off to Chennai for a high-level meeting," Rajesh announced. "She even packed a box of theplas for the trip. You'd think I was headed for a war zone."

The three of them burst into laughter. "You've trained her well," Ankit said, shaking his head.

Finally, Amit arrived, as dramatic as ever. His deep voice and confident stride turned heads wherever he went, and his larger-than-life personality often got them into—and out of—trouble.

"Sorry, boys," Amit said, pulling up a chair. "Got held up. Had to fake some emails to make my leave request look legit. What's the plan?"

"Same as always," Ankit replied. "Meet at Lucknow Airport, fly to Goa, and let the madness begin."

The tea stall buzzed with chatter as Ramu shuffled between tables, serving steaming glasses of chai and plates of crispy samosas. Ankit leaned back in his chair, savoring the sweet, earthy aroma of the tea. Around them, the fading sunlight cast long shadows over the bustling streets of Civil Lines.

"Alright, let's get this straight," Amit said, his tone commanding as he leaned forward. "Who's handling the booze this time? Last year, Sandeep picked the cheapest stuff, and we all woke up with splitting headaches."

"Hey!" Sandeep protested, setting down his glass. "It wasn't cheap, it was... affordable."

"Affordable my foot," Rajesh said, chuckling. "That vodka tasted like paint thinner. This year, Amit's in charge. The guy's got an expensive taste—might as well put it to good use."

Amit grinned and raised his glass in a mock salute. "Leave it to me, boys. This time, we're drinking like kings. No compromises."

"Speaking of compromises," Rajesh said, his tone suddenly serious, "we need to talk about the budget. Last time, we went way overboard. Airbnb, clubs, cab rides—everything costs more now."

"Budget?" Ankit laughed, shaking his head. "You sound like you're planning a family vacation. This is Goa, Rajesh. Budgets don't exist there."

Sandeep, who had been quiet for a while, chimed in hesitantly. "Still, we should keep track. Shalini always asks me about my expenses when I get back. I don't know how to explain why I withdrew so much cash."

Amit rolled his eyes. "Tell her you paid for a team dinner. Or bought gifts for your boss. Be creative, yaar."

The group laughed, but the conversation soon shifted to logistics. Rajesh pulled out his phone and opened a document labeled *Operation Goa 2024*.

"Here's the itinerary," he said, scrolling through the list. "We land at 2 PM. Check-in at the flat by 3:30. First night, we hit Tito's Lane. There's a new club I've been reading about—supposedly the hottest spot right now."

"Great," Ankit said, nodding. "What about the next day? Beach or pool?"

"Beach in the morning," Rajesh replied, "but let's not forget why we're really there."

The table fell silent for a moment, a mischievous grin spreading across Amit's face. "Ah, yes. The annual tradition," he said, raising his eyebrows suggestively.

Sandeep flushed, looking away. Ankit chuckled, leaning back in his chair. "Alright, let's not get ahead of ourselves. One night at a time."

The conversation subsided, and for a moment, they all sat in silence, sipping chai.

"Honestly," Rajesh said, breaking the silence," these trips are the only thing keeping me sane. A week of carefree life is where I feel alive."

Sandeep nodded slowly, "Life with Shalini is new, and I don't know how to fully accept it. I miss the freedom. Just doing something recklessly without thinking about the consequences. And Goa is the perfect place."

Amit leaned back and said," This isn't about Goa, its proving that we still got what it takes."

As the evening wore on, they relaxed, their laughter and camaraderie drawing curious glances from the other patrons. For a moment, they forgot about the lies they'd told and the responsibilities they'd left behind. Here, at this tea stall, they were just four friends, planning an adventure that felt both reckless and liberating.

Eventually, the group dispersed, each heading home to their carefully crafted deceptions.

Ankit's Home: Balancing Guilt and Excitement

Back at home, Ankit found Neha seated on the living room sofa, her laptop open and a cup of coffee by her side. She glanced up as he walked in.

"You're late," she said, her tone matter-of-fact.

"Had to finish some work," Ankit replied, setting his bag down and loosening his tie. He leaned over to kiss her forehead. "Busy day."

Neha closed her laptop and gave him a skeptical look. "You're sure you're not overworking yourself? You've been so distracted lately."

Ankit hesitated for a fraction of a second before forcing a smile. "It's nothing, really. Just a lot of responsibilities at the office."

Their younger son, Aarav, bounded into the room, clutching a toy car. "Papa! Mumma said you're going to Chennai tomorrow. Why?"

Ankit crouched down, ruffling Aarav's hair. "It's work, beta. Grown-up stuff. But I'll be back soon, and I'll bring you a surprise."

"Promise?" Aarav asked, his eyes lighting up.

"Promise," Ankit said, smiling.

Satisfied, Aarav walked away. Neha watched the exchange quietly, her expression softening. "Alright," she said after a moment. "But call me every night, okay? And don't skip meals. You know how you get when you travel."

Ankit nodded, guilt flickering briefly before being replaced by anticipation. He had mastered the art of deception over the years, justifying it as a necessary escape. This was his one week of freedom—a chance to feel alive again.

Amit's Home: The Confident Escape Artist

Meanwhile, Amit walked into his house with a swagger of a man who rehearsed every excuse in his bag. His wife, Shweta, was seated at the dining table, scrolling through her phone.

"You're going to Chennai tomorrow?" She asked without looking up.

"Yep," Amit said, grabbing a glass of water. "Urgent training session. Won't take more than a few days."

Shweta raised an eyebrow. "Training? At your age?"

"It's for the juniors," Amit replied smoothly, sitting down across from her. "I'm supposed to mentor them. Can't say no."

Shweta shrugged, clearly uninterested. "Fine. Just don't forget to call. And remember, you are not young as your juniors, so behave like that. Take your medicines at time and the moment you feel that chest pain again consult the local doctor immediately.."

Amit nodded. "Noted, madam."

Of all the friends, Amit had the easiest time spinning stories. Shweta was too preoccupied with her own work and social circle to dig deeper. For Amit, the lies came naturally, almost like a game.

The Train to Lucknow: On the Verge of Freedom

Two days later, the four friends found themselves aboard a train to Lucknow, their excitement building with every mile.

Ankit sat by the window, watching the fields blur past, his mind already in Goa. Rajesh leaned against the seat, scrolling through his phone and grinning at memes he occasionally shared with the group.

Amit, as usual, was the loudest, regaling them with stories of his previous office antics. "So, this intern," he said, laughing, "thought Excel could calculate emotions. I nearly fell off my chair."

Sandeep, seated beside him, chuckled nervously, still clutching his phone. "Shalini's been texting me nonstop," he muttered. "What if she calls while we're there?"

"Block her," Amit said casually, earning a horrified look from Sandeep. "Relax, I'm joking. Just turn off your phone during the fun stuff."

"I'll say it got stolen," Sandeep said, his tone half-serious.

Rajesh, unable to resist, chimed in," Say you got yourself on a spiritual journey. 'Finding yourself' is always a good excuse."

The group laughed, their camaraderie dispelling any lingering nerves. Outside, the train sped through the countryside, carrying them closer to their secret escape.

CHAPTER 2

The Flight to Freedom

The bustling Lucknow airport was alive with a chaotic symphony of announcements, hurried footsteps, and clatter of trolley wheels rattling on the tiled floor. Ankit and Rajesh did security check-in first, each with a small carry-on bag, and grabbed a corner table at a coffee shop.

"Feels good to finally break free," Rajesh said, sipping his cappuccino, his face lighting up with boyish grin.

"You're telling me," Ankit replied, checking his watch. "Where are Amit and Sandeep? Why do they have to carry so much baggage that they have to check in every time? We're cutting it close."

As if on cue, Amit strode into view, wheeling his suitcase with a confidence that turned a few heads. He was dressed sharply, as if heading to a corporate meeting, and carried a leather duffel bag slung over one shoulder. Sandeep trailed behind him, visibly anxious and clutching his boarding pass as it might disappear.

"About time!" Rajesh called out as they approached. "Thought you two were about to miss the flight."

"Relax, the flight's delayed by 20 minutes," Amit said, tossing his bag onto an empty chair. "Checked the app on the way."

Sandeep sank into a seat, wiping sweat off his forehead. "There was a long queue at the baggage counter. Shalini kept calling. I almost thought—"

"Breathe, kid," Amit interrupted. "You made it. That's what counts."

Rajesh smirked. "He'll calm down after his first drink in Goa."

Sandeep shot him a weak smile. "Let's hope so."

The flight to Goa was uneventful but filled with nervous energy. As the plane taxied down the runway, Ankit stared out the window, watching Lucknow shrink below him. A familiar sense of liberation washed over him—no deadlines, no school pick-ups, no family drama—just the promise of sun, sand, and chaos.

Rajesh, seated beside him, leaned over. "You ever think about how much we risk for this trip?"

Ankit chuckled. "All the time. But the risk makes it worth it, doesn't it?"

Rajesh nodded, a glint of mischief in his eyes. "Every single time."

CHAPTER 3

The Arrival in Goa

The plane touched down in Goa, its wheels skimming across the tarmac with a hum that vibrated deep into their bones. As the plane stopped Amit shouted - Boys, the moment we all been waiting for has arrived.

Their bags were packed with more than just clothes; they carried with them the weight of their lies, the excitement of their secret, and the unspoken tension of what would unfold in the coming days. This trip, like every other, was meant to be their escape—away from the responsibilities, the expectations, and the monotonous grind of their everyday lives in Kanpur.

They had told their families it was a business trip to Chennai, but in truth, they had boarded the flight to Goa, a place they had frequented countless times over the years, but this time, with a different vibe. There were no longer just the typical beach parties or sunset beers; this time, it felt like they were escaping into a world of indulgence, a world where their only boundaries were the ones they set themselves.

The Rush of Arrival

The Goa Airport was bustling with tourists, the air thick with the smell of salty sea breeze and the promise of a carefree holiday. The heat of the afternoon sun hit them as soon as they stepped off the plane. It felt different from Kanpur's dry, dusty air; here, there was a palpable sense of freedom. Amit, the most level-headed of the group, felt a surge of anticipation rise within him. It was as if the moment they landed, all the pressures of home, work, and family were suddenly behind them.

Rajesh, always the first to take charge, stepped forward with the confident swagger of someone who had done this a thousand times. "Let's grab a cab, get to the flat, and get this trip started the right way," he said, already pulling up the app to order a ride.

Ankit, who had been quieter than usual, turned to Sandeep with a grin. "I can't believe we're finally here. No family, no work, just us. The old us," he said, his voice low but charged with excitement.

Sandeep let out a loud laugh. "You're right. No ties, no responsibilities. Just fun. It's been too long since we've done this."

They piled into the cab, a beat-up Maruti Suzuki van with colorful beaded seat cover was filled with faint fish aroma. The driver, a man with a thick mustache and a laid-back demeanor, took them through the winding roads of Goa, the palm trees swaying in the breeze, and the coastal scenery flashing by in a blur. The sound of the waves crashing on the shore was a constant background hum, a reminder that they were at the edge of the world, far from their usual lives.

As the cab sped towards the flat, they had rented through Airbnb, Amit looked out the window, thinking back to their previous trips to Goa. Each year, it had been a wild, carefree adventure. The memories blurred together—endless nights of drinking, clubbing, and meeting strangers. But they were older now, in their late thirties, with more baggage—both emotional and physical. This wasn't just another trip; it was a statement. They were still young at heart, still capable of the wild abandon they had once known.

The Villa in the Heart of Goa

Their Villa was located in a quieter area of the city, tucked away from the madness of the tourist hotspots, but still close enough to the action. It was spacious, modern, and beautifully furnished, with a large balcony overlooking a patch of green. The apartment had a cool, coastal vibe—seafoam-colored walls, wicker furniture, and soft, patterned rugs. It was a far cry from the small, cramped hotel rooms they had stayed in on previous trips.

As they entered, the cool air of the flat wrapped around them like a welcoming embrace. Amit dropped his bag by the door, taking a deep breath. "This is it," he said, smiling. "Let's make this trip count."

Ankit immediately flopped onto the couch, his legs stretched out in front of him. "I can't wait to hit the beach. Let's get a few drinks first, though, right? Warm up to the madness."

Sandeep didn't need reminders. He opened the minibar and pulled out a bottle of rum. "Hell yes," he said, pouring generous amounts into four glasses. "We need to kick things off right. To Goa and to us—old school style."

They clinked their glasses, the ice cubes rattling, as the sharp taste of alcohol hit their throats. The warmth of the rum mixed with the heat outside, filling them with a sense of nostalgia for the old days. There was a moment of silence as they all sipped their drinks, reflecting on how things had changed.

Rajesh broke the silence, his voice playful yet conspiratorial. "You guys know what we need now, don't you?"

Rajesh's grin widened. "I'm talking about the clubs, the real Goa experience. But not just any clubs. We're going to Tito's Lane tonight. Get ready for some wild fun."

As the night approached, the excitement in the flat was palpable. They got ready, each of them dressing to impress. The mirror in the bathroom reflected their eager faces, younger versions of themselves, the men they had once been. They weren't businessmen, fathers, or husbands tonight. They were just four friends on a mission to enjoy the pleasures of life without restraint.

CHAPTER 4

Tito's Lane and Temptation

The night was alive in Tito's Lane, an iconic stretch in the heart of Goa where revelers from all walks of life mingled, danced, and lost themselves in the pulsing beats of thumping house music. The lane was lit with neon signs advertising the hottest clubs, bars, and—most importantly—endless nights of indulgence. The air was thick with the mingling scents of sizzling street food, sweet perfumes, and the faint aroma of the ocean that seemed to call out from the distance.

Amit, Ankit, Rajesh, and Sandeep stood at the entrance of the lane, feeling the energy hit them like a tidal wave. It was as if they had stepped into another world—a world where rules didn't exist, where everyone was a stranger, and where only the moment mattered. It was almost overwhelming— the music roaring from every direction, the laughter, the dance, the clink of glasses, the hum of people who left their lives outside this magical place.

There was a dangerous, almost intoxicating tension in the air. Perhaps it was the alcohol still warming their insides, or maybe it was the sense of freedom they felt after leaving behind their regular lives in Kanpur. Whatever it was, they were ready to let go completely.

"Alright, boys, this is it," Rajesh said, his voice full of mischief. "We've had enough talking about the old days and reflecting on our lives. Tonight, we're going to go all in. No holding back."

Amit raised his glass, his eyes gleaming with excitement. "Let's make it count."

Sandeep, as always, grinned broadly. "Exactly. Let's get wild, just like we used to."

Ankit, raised an eyebrow, couldn't help but smile at their enthusiasm. "You guys sure about this?

Rajesh slapped him on the back. "Come on, Amit. A little fun won't hurt. We're not changing forever—just taking a break from all the responsibilities. Tonight, we do whatever we want. You in?"

Ankit hesitated, but then the music in the distance, the lights, and the crowd's energy pulled him in. "Alright," he said, smiling. "Let's go."

The group made their way to the club, weaving through the crowd. Scooters zipped past occasionally, their engines roaring above the music, carrying tourists all around the world. Some hailed down form the cab, arguing with the drivers. The vendors hawked everything from local dishes to shawarma's. The men paused to grab some quick kebabs, the spicy flavor adding up to their already growing adrenaline.

The Clubbing Scene

The moment they stepped inside, it hit them: The sound of bass-heavy music thudded from inside, music and energy drawing them closer. The rush of cool air and strobe lights enveloped them. It was an assault on the senses: flashing lights, the smell of perfume and sweat, and the bass vibrating through their bodies.

The club was packed with people, all lost in the rhythm of the music. Some danced wildly on the floor, others lounged at the bar, chatting with strangers, their faces illuminated by neon glow. The energy in the air was enlightening, and the men couldn't help but feel it. For once, they weren't employees, fathers, or husbands— they were just four men out for a night of unbridled fun.

Rajesh immediately made a beeline for the bar. "Shots first," he declared, flashing a grin. "The night is young."

The bartender, with spectacles and warm smile, lined up the tequila shots with precision of a surgeon. Salt, lime, liquor— the ritual of Goa's nightlife.

Ankit, seemed to catch the same contagious energy. "To the night."

Sandeep, already feeling the buzz from the rum they had drunk earlier, joined in. "To Goa."

Amit followed, smiling at the carefree energy around them. The shots burned in their throats, but they didn't care. It felt liberating. They ordered round after round, the alcohol flowing freely. Each shot seemed to loosen them up more, pulling them deeper into the wild atmosphere of the club.

The Tempting Distractions

As the night wore on, Amit noticed the growing crowd of women around them. Goa, with its exotic charm and liberal atmosphere, attracted all kinds of people—tourists, locals, partygoers, and, of course, the occasional escort looking for wealthy clients to entertain. The four men had seen it all before, but tonight, there was something different in the air.

It wasn't just the usual women flirting for attention or trying to score free drinks. No, tonight, the women seemed more forward, more enticing. Amit noticed a few glances in their direction—flirtatious looks, smiles that promised more than just a casual conversation. He felt the temptation rise within him.

Sandeep, who had been eyeing a group of women by the dance floor, leaned toward Amit and whispered, "You see those girls? They've been checking us out all night. I think they're looking for a little fun."

Rajesh overheard and laughed. "What do you think, Amit? Should we invite them over for a drink? Show them what Kanpur guys are made of?"

Ankit looked at his friends and then scanned the crowd. He caught one of the women looking at him, her smile playful and inviting. He wasn't usually one to dive into risky situations, but tonight, something felt different. Maybe it was the alcohol, or maybe it was the allure of the night, but he found himself drawn to the idea.

Amit, despite the little voice of caution in his head, found himself nodding. "I guess it wouldn't hurt to have a little fun."

CHAPTER 5

Svetlana and Nadya: The Deal

The neon haze of Tito's Lane painted everything in vibrant streaks of red and blue, pulsing in time with the pounding bass that spilled from every open doorway. The sticky Goan air carried a cocktail of sensations—sea salt, sweat, and the faint tang of spilled drinks—making the scene feel loud, alive, and just a touch overwhelming.

Amit, Ankit, Rajesh, and Sandeep wove through the crowd of revelers, dodging the occasional bump of a shoulder or burst of raucous laughter. Somewhere near the bar, they'd spotted them—the women. Their laughter, sharp and melodic, had managed to cut through the chaotic soundscape, freezing the group mid-step as they exchanged quick, wordless glances.

Now, as they closed in, the tension among them was undeniable. Amit tugged at the damp collar of his linen shirt and cleared his throat, breaking the awkward silence. "So... what's the plan?" he asked, voice low enough to be swallowed by the music if not for the charged quiet between them.

"Plan?" Ankit snorted, though the fidgeting fingers at the edge of his watch betrayed his nerves. "We just talk. How hard can it be?"

"You mean like last time? When you 'just talked' and ended up ordering three shots because you blanked out mid-sentence?" Rajesh countered, his tone bone-dry as he adjusted his footing, sand still clinging to their shoes.

Sandeep, ever the silent observer, chuckled softly but stayed focused on the bar. His gaze lingered on the two women. One leaned against the counter, her back to them, a cascade of dark hair cascading over her shoulders, while the other gestured animatedly, her laughter drawing curious looks from nearby strangers.

As the group closed the gap, the atmosphere shifted. The music felt louder now, almost intrusive, its relentless beat syncing uncomfortably with the thundering rhythm in their chests.

"What's the worst that could happen?" Amit muttered, more to himself than the others, like he was trying to will the words into courage.

"They could ignore us," Sandeep finally said, his tone flat but cutting. "Or worse, laugh at us."

"Fantastic pep talk," Ankit muttered with an exaggerated eye roll.

Just then, one of the women turned slightly in their direction, their movements slow and unhurried. One of them locked eyes with Rajesh, just for a fleeting moment. Something unreadable—curiosity, maybe—flashed in her expression before she turned back to her friend.

"Well, boys," Amit said, forcing a grin as he straightened his shoulders, "we didn't come all the way to Goa just to chicken out. Go, Rajesh, go…"

Rajesh grinned, brushing off the nerves like dust from his shoes," Watch and learn, boys."

And with a mix of shaky resolve, the group finally closed the distance.

Rajesh led the charge, sliding up with a swagger that was shy of cocky. With his charm, he struck up a conversation with two women sitting by the bar. They were both tall, strikingly beautiful, and appeared to be in their late twenties—foreign, their accents thick and exotic.

Rajesh, sensing an opportunity for excitement, didn't shy away from the conversation. He leaned in close, flashing his signature grin. "Mind if we join you?" He asked, his voice low and filled with intrigue.

The taller of the two, smiled seductively. Her eyes sparkled in the dim light, and she held his gaze without hesitation. "Depends. You buying the next round? "She replied, her voice smooth and confident.

Rajesh shot back," Depends. What are we drinking?"

"Vodka," she said," Always Vodka."

The group eased into the conversation. Their names, as it turned out, were Svetlana and Nadya. They were both Ukrainian escorts working the club scene, a fact they made no attempt to hide.

Ankit and Sandeep, sensing the turn in the conversation, joined them at the bar. They all exchanged glances, a shared understanding passing between them. This wasn't just another night out—they were stepping into something they hadn't experienced before. It felt so... deliberate.

"What brings you here?" Nadya asked, her blonde hair shimmering under the club lights.

Rajesh shrugged," Just looking for some good time. Thought Tito's Lane the place to be."

"You heard right" Svetlana said, her smile seductive," You have come to the right place. We will make your night unforgettable."

As the conversation shifted from casual to more suggestive, Svetlana and Nadya leaned in closer. They spoke with the kind of confidence that suggested they had done this many times before. The group of friends was intrigued, unsure of what to expect but undeniably drawn to the offer they were being presented with.

Rajesh leaned closer, "Define unforgettable?"

Svetlana, ever the professional, was quick to lay out the details. "For tonight," she began, "we're offering a full-service experience. The night will be yours to do with as you please. A little fun, a little indulgence, and, if you're up for it, we'll make sure it's a night you'll never forget."

Nadya nodded in agreement. "It's a flat rate for the whole night. No surprises. You'll get our full attention, no interruptions."

Rajesh, already thinking about how to make the most of this, asked the obvious question. "What's the price for the night? And what exactly does that cover?"

Svetlana smiled slyly. "For all four of you, 15,000 each. Full service. We'll take care of everything. But, of course, there are... options for extra services if you want to go beyond the basics." Her eyes glinted with a hint of mystery, as if daring them to take the plunge into deeper waters.

The price wasn't exactly cheap, but given their current mood and the thrill of the moment, none of the men hesitated. Rajesh quickly pulled out his phone to arrange the details, eager to make the night unforgettable.

"Done," Rajesh said with a wink, signaling to the others. "We're in."

The women smiled, clearly pleased with the agreement. "We'll meet you outside in an hour," Nadya said. "Enjoy the rest of your drinks, and we'll be ready when you are."

With that, Svetlana and Nadya gracefully left the bar, walking away with the sort of poise that told the men this was just another night of work for them. But for Amit, Ankit, Rajesh, and Sandeep, it felt like the beginning of something far more thrilling—an adventure they hadn't fully anticipated but were eager to dive into.

The Waiting Game

As the women walked away, the excitement among the men was at it's peak. Rajesh was practically buzzing with excitement, his mind already racing with possibilities. Sandeep was grinning like a Cheshire cat, while Ankit looked more hesitant, though still intrigued by what was about to unfold.

Amit, however, felt a mix of anticipation and unease. He had always been the more responsible one, the one who had balanced the wild times of the past with the realities of adulthood. But even he couldn't deny the pull of temptation tonight. Something about this trip, this escape, made him feel like he could let go, just for a little while.

"So," Ankit began, breaking the silence as they sipped their drinks, "we've already agreed on the price, are we really doing this?"

Rajesh chuckled. "What do you mean? This is Goa, Ankit. We've been here before. You know how it goes. Tonight, we'll live it up. No rules, no consequences."

Sandeep nodded enthusiastically. "Exactly! This is just another level of fun. We're in the right place at the right time. The kind of fun we used to have back in the day, remember?"

Ankit, still a little hesitant, shrugged. "Yeah, but this feels different. I mean, we're paying for—"

"Relax, Ankit," Rajesh interrupted with a dismissive wave. "We've got the money. It's just about enjoying the moment. Don't overthink it. Think of it like an experience."

Amit knew Rajesh was right in a way. It was just an experience, just another night in Goa where the rules didn't apply. The question was, how far would they take it? Would they truly let go, or would they hold back, never fully embracing the reckless freedom they had come here for?

The Wild Turn

The anticipation in the air grew thicker as the hour passed. The group could feel the weight of their decision growing with every tick of the clock. When the time came to leave the club and meet Svetlana and Nadya, the group was ready. They piled into a cab, heading toward a private villa they had arranged for the night.

The car ride was filled with nervous excitement, each man lost in his thoughts about what awaited them.

As they reached the villa, the mood shifted from playful curiosity to something much more intense. The house was secluded, far from the buzzing nightlife of the main tourist areas. It was quiet, almost eerie in its calmness, a stark contrast to the wild energy of the club.

Svetlana and Nadya were already waiting for them, standing at the entrance, their eyes glimmering with knowing smiles. The deal had been made, and now it was time for the night to unfold.

"Ready?" Svetlana asked, her voice carrying a challenge.

With a deep breath, Rajesh stepped forward, his usual confidence unwavering. "Let's do this," he said, smiling at his friends.

And just like that, the line between indulgence and excess began to blur.

CHAPTER 6

The Wild Night Gone Wrong

The air inside the villa was thick with the musky scent of perfume, the faint trace of alcohol, and the nervous energy that crackled between Amit, Ankit, Rajesh, and Sandeep. The night had begun with a sense of freedom—an escape from their regular lives, a break from responsibility. But as they stood in the dimly lit living room of the private villa, surrounded by Svetlana and Nadya, the atmosphere was charged with a different kind of anticipation. The line between fun and recklessness was about to be crossed, and no one knew just how far they'd go.

Svetlana and Nadya had already made themselves comfortable, seated on the plush couches in the living room. The two women exuded confidence, each in her own way—Svetlana with her dark, sultry eyes that seemed to pierce through the men, and Nadya, with her playful smile and flirtatious demeanor. The two of them had made it clear that this night was all about pleasure, indulgence, and living in the moment.

Rajesh, his usual bold self, clapped his hands. "Alright, ladies. You know what we're here for. Let's get this party started, shall we?"

Svetlana smiled wickedly. "Of course, darling. But first, why don't you all relax a little? We'll take care of the rest."

With a flick of her wrist, she gestured for the men to take a seat. As they did, Svetlana and Nadya began to pour drinks—rich, dark rum mixed with cola, an enticing cocktail that slid smoothly down their throats. The alcohol began to flow freely, loosening their inhibitions and heightening the buzz that had already started in their veins.

Sandeep, grinning like he'd hit the jackpot, raised his glass, "This is going to be one hell of a night, boys. Just wait."

The Beginning of the Chaos

It didn't take long for things to spiral. The initial moments were filled with lighthearted laughter and playful teasing. Svetlana and Nadya expertly played their roles—charming, alluring, and incredibly skilled at making the men feel like the center of attention. The alcohol flowed freely, and with each drink, the night seemed to get wilder.

Rajesh leaned in toward Svetlana, his hands brushing against her as he whispered something in her ear. She responded with a smile that promised everything—and nothing. There was an unspoken understanding between them: tonight was about pushing limits.

Ankit found himself drawn into Nadya's playful charm. The temptation to let go and lose himself in the madness was growing stronger with each passing minute. Amit, too, had been drawn into the chaos, his earlier hesitations fading as the night wore on.

But it was Sandeep, as usual, who took things too far. He made his way over to Nadya, pulling her close in a way that seemed almost predatory. Nadya didn't resist; instead, she seemed to enjoy the attention, leading Sandeep into a private corner of the villa.

"Easy there, Romeo", Rajesh countered, as he watched them disappear.

Amid the laughter and clinking glasses, Amit found himself shuffling through his bag. His heart pounding, he didn't know if it was the alcohol or the anticipation in the air. Pulling out his medicine, he swallowed a pill quickly. The banter momentarily helped the unease gnawing at him.

The Moment of No Return

As the night wore on, the group became more and more immersed in the frenzy of the evening. The music, the alcohol, and the sensual promises of Svetlana and Nadya all blurred into one intoxicating mix. The villa's living room became a playground for indulgence—laughter mixed with the sound of clinking glasses, the occasional moan of pleasure, and the faint rustle of clothing.

It started with a whisper from Nadya, who pulled Amit aside when he wasn't paying attention. "You sure you want to keep going like this?" she asked, her tone suddenly serious.

Amit, his senses clouded by alcohol, frowned. "What do you mean?"

She smirked, brushing a strand of hair behind her ear. "You're not the type to do things like this, are you? There's no turning back, you know."

The comment struck a nerve, but Amit tried to brush it off. He had come this far—what was the harm in going a little further?

He laughed nervously, waving her off," You're overthinking it."

Her eyes lingered on him for a moment, as if to say, *you will see.*

But that's when things started to spiral.

The Break in Trust

Out of nowhere, the door to the villa burst open. It was an unexpected intrusion—an aggressive pounding, followed by the unmistakable sound of heavy footsteps. Svetlana and Nadya exchanged panicked glances. The mood shifted instantly, and the confident, flirtatious atmosphere that had hung over the room now felt tense and uneasy.

Rajesh, who had been in the midst of enjoying the attention, looked up, confused. "What the hell?"

Before anyone could respond, the door swung open, revealing two burly men—goons, for lack of a better word. They stormed into the room, their eyes scanning the area as they looked around. The tension in the air was palpable.

"Where are they?" One of the men barked, his voice full of authority. "Svetlana. Nadya."

Nadya quickly jumped to her feet, her face draining of color. she muttered something under her breath. Svetlana, too, seemed to recognize the danger, but her calm demeanor gave nothing away.

The men didn't seem to care about pleasantries. One of them grabbed Nadya roughly by the arm. "You've been skimming off the top, haven't you?" he hissed, his tone cold.

Amit, who had been standing at the edge of the room, realized what was happening. This wasn't just a regular escort job. This was something darker. These women weren't just offering pleasure—they were part of a larger, dangerous operation, and the men were here to collect.

Rajesh, whose confidence was shattered, tried to reason with the goons. "Wait, we paid for everything. We've already settled the amount— 15,000 each. There must be some misunderstanding."

The larger goon laughed bitterly. "Do you think this is about money?" He spat. "You were part of the plan. You paid up, and now you're going to pay again. This is a lesson."

The Scam Unravels

As the chaos continued to escalate, the situation became clear: Svetlana and Nadya had scammed them. The night that had started as an escape had suddenly turned into a nightmare. Amit felt the pieces falling into the place— the women's bold approach, Nadya's cryptic warning and the outlandish price they had agreed to pay. The men—naive and caught up in the heat of the moment—hadn't even realized they had been tricked.

Amit, his heart racing, could feel the panic setting in. Amit turned to Ankit and said- 'This wasn't supposed to happen.'

Both Sandeep and Ankit soon realized what was happening as their blood flow changed it's direction and started flowing back to their brains.

Sandeep drenched in sweat said - 'Bro Shalini will kill me if she finds out.'

Ankit looked at Sandeep and angrily said- 'You think our wives will give us medals you idiot.'

Meanwhile, Amit mind raced with questions. Approaching Svetlana and Nadya was way too easy. Everything went down smoothly until now. The pounding on door was not accidental, the goons had tacked them down.

"How did they find this place?" Sandeep whispered, his voice laced with panic.

"They must have tracked Svetlana and Nadya. Maybe a phone call or GPS." Amit replied, realization dawning at him.

"We won't leave until you pay us up. If you try to escape or worse, you will not leave this place alive," their leader said, his expression menacing.

Before anyone could respond, the goons, Svetlana and Nadya disappeared into the back rooms of the villa, pouring themselves a rigorous amount of alcohol, leaving the men to deal with the situation they had unknowingly walked into.

CHAPTER 7

The Chaos

The once-luxurious villa now felt like a trap. The bright lights of Goa's infamous nightclubs seemed light years away, and the sounds of laughter and music had faded into the dark corners of Amit's mind. Instead, a strange, suffocating silence had settled over the group. The air was thick with tension, regret, and a sense of impending doom.

The four friends, still reeling from the shock of the earlier confrontation with the goons, stood in the living room, looking at each other with wide eyes. Rajesh, always the instigator, looked unsettled for the first time in years. His usual bravado had evaporated, replaced by a nervous energy that betrayed the deep unease creeping into his soul.

"Do you think they'll come after us?" Sandeep asked, his voice low and filled with concern. He paced back and forth, his face etched with anxiety.

Amit, his hands clenched into fists, couldn't shake the fear gnawing at him. "I don't know. But something tells me this isn't over. We just got caught up in something way bigger than we realized."

Ankit stood by the window, peering out into the darkness, his eyes scanning the empty street. The place was quiet, save for the distant hum of engine. "It's not just the goons I'm worried about," he said quietly. "There's a vehicle heading our way. What if they come here? What if they've already got their eyes on us?"

Rajesh was starting to lose his usual calm. "We've got no time to waste. We need to leave, now. We need to get out of here before things get worse."

As if on cue, the sound of approaching sirens pierced the night air. The distant wail grew louder, and suddenly, the sound of a car screeching to a halt outside the villa rang in their ears, signaling the arrival of law enforcement.

The Arrival of the Police

"Shit," Rajesh muttered under his breath, his face pale. "They're here."

The men froze. Panic spread like wildfire through their veins. Amit's heart was pounding in his chest, and his mind raced. They hadn't done anything illegal, at least not that they could pinpoint, but in Goa's lawless underbelly, who could say what might come of this?

Sandeep spoke in a hushed tone, his eyes darting around. "We've got to get out. Now."

But it was too late. A handful of uniformed officers stormed in, their heavy boots thudding against the marble floor. The men didn't need to see their badges to know they weren't the average local police. These officers had the hard, cold look of men who didn't answer to anyone.

The leader of the group, a tall, broad-shouldered officer with a scar running down his cheek, stepped forward. His eyes scanned the room, taking in the four men with sharp scrutiny. "What the hell is going on here?" He barked.

Before the men could respond, Svetlana and Nadya, who had reappeared after disappearing into the back rooms during the chaos, were standing behind the officers, their faces pale and guarded. There was no longer any trace of the sultry charm they had exuded earlier; now, they were merely shadows of their former selves, caught up in something far darker.

Rajesh, trying to regain some semblance of control, stepped forward. "We... we were just having a good time. Nothing illegal here. Just enjoying our vacation."

The officer didn't seem convinced. His eyes narrowed, and he turned to his men. "Search the place," he ordered, his voice clipped. "They've got something to hide."

The Goons' Return

As the officers began searching the villa, the tension mounted. The men's hearts raced as they watched the police rifle through the rooms, opening drawers, flipping through bags, and pulling apart suitcases. It felt like the walls were closing in, the overwhelming sense of doom creeping over them like a thick fog.

But just as things seemed to reach their peak, the two goons from earlier, the ones who had stormed in with the rage and cold anger of men who had nothing left to lose, walked in without a care. They weren't alone this time.

The officers immediately stiffened, recognizing the third men, and a strange, silent understanding passed between them. The goons were not to be messed with. As they made their way toward the men, the tension in the room grew even more unbearable.

"You think you can escape from us?" The larger of the two goons sneered at the men, his face twisted with a malevolent grin.

"I told you," the other goon growled. "You can't hide from us. Now it's time to pay up."

The police officers, who had been busy searching, stopped what they were doing and turned their attention toward the newcomers. Their faces were filled with resignation, as though they had seen this play before.

"What is happening in here? You think I don't know what you are doing here" The officer demanded.

"It's our business officer. You know how it is."

"It is our business, you know I have to take action if they file a complaint."

The leader looked at the men and sneered.

"This is your last warning." The tall officer said, turning to the girls. "You're in deep now. There's nothing you can do to fix this. Either way, we are not cleaning up your mess."

The situation was spinning out of control. Amit, Ankit, Rajesh, and Sandeep stood helplessly; caught in the crossfire of a dangerous game they hadn't fully understood when they first stepped into the villa.

A Deal with the Devil

Amit felt the weight of the room pressing down on him. The tension between them were palpable, making one thing clear: this was not a fight between crime and justice. It was a power play and they had walked straight into the trap.

In a swift move, the officer stepped toward Rajesh, his gaze fixed and unblinking. "You men have no idea what kind of trouble you've walked into, do you?" he asked, his voice tinged with disdain. "This is Goa's underbelly. You're not just dealing with the cops here. You're dealing with people who can make you disappear fast."

Rajesh, swallowing hard, opened his mouth to speak, but the words failed him. He had no idea how things had gotten so far. The situation was rapidly unraveling, and now the officers seemed more like enforcers of a corrupt system than agents of law and order.

Svetlana and Nadya, in a moment of desperation, glanced at each other. Then, as if making a decision in the blink of an eye, they spoke simultaneously. "We'll fix it," Svetlana said, her voice laced with fear. "We'll settle the payments. We'll take care of everything. Just let them go."

Nadya nodded quickly. "Please. We've made a mistake. Let's end this here."

The officer didn't respond immediately, instead looking over at the goons, who were now pacing like hungry wolves circling their prey. The goons, too, were weighing the offer, their expressions unreadable.

A few long moments passed before the officer finally nodded, seemingly satisfied with the resolution. "Fine. You'll pay the price for your mistake. But remember, this is your one chance. We won't tolerate another screw-up."

The goons turned to leave along with Nadya and Svetlana, and as quickly as they had entered, they were gone, vanishing into the night with the air of men who had already claimed their prize.

The police, too, seemed to lose interest in the scene. They gave one last, disdainful glance at the group of men, "You four. Consider yourself lucky. If I see your faces again, you won't be walking out of Goa alive." They too turned to follow the goons out of the villa, leaving the four friends in stunned silence.

The men stood in stunned silence, processing the magnitude of what had just happened. They had been scammed, caught in a dangerous web of deceit and greed. They had crossed a line they hadn't even fully understood—and now, they had to face the consequences.

Rajesh dropped onto the couch, burying his face in his hands, "I... I didn't think it would go this far."

Sandeep, his usual smirk gone, shook his head. "I should have known better. We've been idiots."

Ankit, his voice low. "We were nothing to them, just collateral damage."

Amit, still processing everything, spoke up. "We need to leave. This was a bad idea from the start."

But even as they vacated the villa, the damage to their innocence had been done. The wild night had gone terribly wrong, and as they sat in the cab, speeding away from the scene, one thing was certain:

Their trip to Goa would be remembered for all the wrong reasons.

CHAPTER 8

The Aftermath

The vehicle rolled through the silent Goan night, its stillness amplified by the weight of unanswered questions. The four men—Amit, Ankit, Sandeep, and Rajesh—sat in tense silence, minds racing to piece together the night's events.

"What exactly had happened? How had the goons discovered their location? And where had the police come from to rescue them in the nick of time?

Breaking the quiet, the cab driver—an older man with a weathered face—spoke.

"Sir," he began, glancing at them in the rearview mirror, "It seems you too have been scammed by these foreigners."

Amit, startled by the comment, turned to face him. It took a moment for recognition to dawn. "Wait," Amit said, his voice rising slightly, "You're the same driver who dropped us at the villa earlier, aren't you?"

The driver nodded, a faint smile curling his lips. "Yes, sir. And you're lucky to have gotten out so easily. Those girls? They aren't just escorts. They're drug peddlers."

The revelation struck like lightning. The four men stared at the driver, their earlier exhaustion now replaced by outrage.

"You knew about this the whole time?" Ankit exploded, his voice echoing in the confined space. "And now you're telling us?" Without waiting for a response, he lunged forward, his hands aiming for the driver's collar.

"Relax, sir, relax!" the driver exclaimed, swerving slightly to avoid a pothole.

Sandeep and Rajesh quickly pulled Ankit back into his seat, their combined strength calming the storm—if only for a moment.

The driver exhaled deeply before continuing, his tone firm but apologetic. "I'm just a simple cab driver, sir. I can't afford to go against them. These people are dangerous. Those girls? They lure tourists into their trap. Once the tourists feel comfortable, the girls signal the goons. That's when the real scam begins. They demand payment for drugs the tourists didn't even know existed, and if anyone resists, they don't hesitate to threaten—or worse."

Amit, his temper barely contained, cut him off. "And you still left us there, knowing all this? Were you waiting to collect our dead bodies?" His voice trembled with anger.

"Calm down, sir," the driver said, his tone now tinged with pride. "How do you think the police arrived in time to save you?"

The question hung in the air, momentarily silencing the men.

The driver flicked back between the road and the mirror, his gaze steady. "I may not be strong enough to take them on myself, but as a true Goan, it is my duty to keep tourists safe. After I dropped you at the villa, I recognized the girls and realized you'd been caught in their trap. I immediately called the police and explained everything. They promised to intervene before it was too late."

The tension in the cab began to dissipate. The driver's calm explanation had a disarming effect, and the men's anger morphed into gratitude.

Rajesh, overwhelmed, leaned forward and hugged the driver from behind. "Thank you," he said, his voice choked with emotion. "You saved our lives."

The driver nodded, his face softening. "It's my job, sir. I'm just glad you're all safe."

When they finally reached their new villa, the men stepped out of the cab. Amit dug into his wallet and handed the driver a generous tip, his eyes conveying gratitude beyond words.

"Thank you," Amit said. "We owe you our lives."

The driver tipped his head respectfully. "Enjoy the rest of your stay, sir. Be careful next time."

As the cab drove away, the four men stood in the quiet embrace of their new villa's courtyard. The night, which had seemed endless, had finally drawn to a close.

The villa was eerily quiet the next morning. The rays of the Goa sun filtered through the windows, casting a soft golden glow over the room.

Amit, Ankit, Rajesh, and Sandeep sat in a circle, nursing their sore heads, each of them nursing their own thoughts. The room was still scattered with their packed bags and yet, there was an uneasy calm hanging in the air. The reckless excitement they had once felt seemed like a distant memory now, replaced by a gnawing sense of discomfort and self-reflection.

"Well," Rajesh said finally, breaking the tension, "that was... something."

"Something stupid," Ankit muttered, rubbing his temples. "How did we let this happen?"

Amit sighed. "It's Goa, guys. These things happen. Let's not dwell on it."

Sandeep said quietly, looking at his friends, "We're done, right? We're not doing this again. No more escorts, no more wild nights. This trip has been enough to last a lifetime."

Ankit nodded slowly, his face clouded with guilt. "We've crossed a line we shouldn't have. The police, the goons, everything that went down last night—it's all too much. We've had our fun, but it's over."

Rajesh rubbed his temple and let out a deep sigh. "You're right. We got carried away. This whole thing was supposed to be a break, a getaway. But it turned into something far darker than we ever imagined."

Amit stared at his friends, his eyes filled with a mix of exhaustion and remorse. He had been the one to suggest this trip in the first place, and now, sitting in the villa, surrounded by the remnants of their hedonistic indulgence, he felt the weight of their actions pressing on him. "Maybe we've all lost it a little," he murmured. "Maybe we needed to stop before things went too far."

For a moment, it seemed as though they were all in agreement. The night had gone horribly wrong, and they all acknowledged the chaos they had caused. But the familiar taste of alcohol—still lingering on their breath and in their veins—had a different effect than they expected. It didn't make them more somber or introspective. Instead, it stirred something else.

Sandeep, who had been nervous since last night, suddenly stood up. "I'm going for a walk," he said, his voice tight.

"Let him go," Amit said when Ankit moved to follow him. "He'll come around. He always does."

The sun was high, the sky impossibly blue, and the air thick with the scent of salt and sunscreen. Goa, with its endless stretches of beach, felt like a paradise—one that, for the moment, seemed untouched by the chaos of last night.

Ankit, Rajesh, and Amit made their way to Baga Beach, leaving Sandeep behind in the villa, still nursing the aftermath of the previous night. The other three had decided that a little time in the sun and the sound of the waves might help them reset, away from the stressful tension of the night before.

Baga Beach was already lively, even at midmorning. Paragliders dotted the sky, their colorful sails popping against the clear expanse of blue. Young couples walked hand-in-hand along the shore, their footprints disappearing into the sand with each crashing wave. Local vendors called out from their stalls, offering everything from beach towels to trinkets.

Rajesh wasted no time in setting up on a nearby beach chair, ordering a cold beer from the vendor that passed by. "This is what life's all about, yaar!" He said, stretching out with a grin.

"Not bad, Rajesh," Ankit agreed, setting his towel down beside him. He kicked off his flip-flops and waded into the shallows, feeling the cool water lap at his feet. He needed the peace, the simple rhythm of the ocean to soothe his nerves. There was a lingering discomfort inside him, a sense of unease from the events of the previous night, but he couldn't shake the excitement of being in Goa.

Amit, who had a more laid-back approach to life, joined Ankit by the water. "You're still thinking about last night, huh?" Amit said, looking out at the horizon. "You can't let it ruin the trip. Let it go."

Ankit glanced at his friend. "I know, but it's hard to ignore, man. We're supposed to be better than this."

Amit shrugged. "You can't change the past. But right now, we're here, and we're not doing anything to get into trouble. Enjoy the beach. Forget the rest for a while."

Ankit smiled weakly, grateful for Amit's reassurance. He followed his friend's lead, shaking off the tension in his shoulders. The beach was a welcome distraction, a place where the world seemed to slow down just enough to take in the beauty around them.

Sandeep's Solitude

Meanwhile, Sandeep remained behind in the villa, nursing a bottle of water and sitting by the open window. He could hear the distant sound of the waves crashing against the shore, but somehow it only reminded him of the noise of last night—the shouting, the panic, the feeling of being caught up in something he didn't want.

He ran his hand through his hair, unsure of where to go from here. He hadn't signed up for any of this. Sure, he had agreed to come along, but all of this—the excess, the wildness—it felt too far removed from his reality. He had never been comfortable with the idea of pushing boundaries, but here he was, caught in the middle of something that made him feel uncomfortable.

He'd never been one to let his guard down easily, not even with his closest friends, but the lies they'd all told their families—his wife, Shalini, in particular—made his stomach turn. Every time her texts or calls popped up on his phone, it reminded him of his double life, and he hated it.

But then again, was this any different from what he did in Kanpur every day? He worked hard to provide for his family and he hardly ever did anything for himself. Maybe this trip—this reckless adventure—was his way of breaking free. Maybe this was the escape he'd needed for a long time, even if it came with consequences.

Sandeep shook his head, banishing the thoughts. "Focus on the present," he whispered to himself.

With a sigh, he stood up, grabbed his sunglasses, and stepped out of the villa, determined to join the others on the beach, if only to distract himself from the heavy weight on his chest.

Reuniting on the Beach

The trio was still lounging when Sandeep arrived, his steps slower, his expression still distant. Rajesh spotted him first and waved him over. "Hey, Sandeep! Join us, man! The water's perfect!"

Sandeep smiled faintly, but hesitated for a moment before trudging over. He stood at the edge of the water, unsure of himself. Amit caught his eye from the beach chair and tossed him a bottle of water.

"Here, have a drink first. You need to hydrate."

Sandeep nodded, unscrewing the cap. "Thanks."

Ankit noticed the tension still in his friend's body and knew that Sandeep wasn't quite there yet. But, for now, they would let it be.

After a few more minutes of silence, Rajesh spoke up again. "You know, I've been thinking. Tonight, we do something different. We hit the beach clubs, but this time, we're just chill. No need to get wrapped up in anything crazy."

"Yeah," Ankit added, nodding. "We can just enjoy ourselves, no need for drama."

Sandeep suddenly broke into a grin. "I can handle that. Just... let's keep it simple, alright?"

Amit grinned, raising his beer in salute. "Simple it is."

The group spent the rest of the afternoon lounging in the sun, laughing about old stories from their school days, poking fun at each other's dancing skills, and finally easing into the rhythm of the Goa beach life. Even Sandeep found himself laughing along with the others, letting the ocean waves wash away some of his discomfort.

As the sun dipped lower, painting the sky with shades of pink and orange, the group stood together and walked down to the water's edge, dipping their toes into the cool tide.

"We came for this," Rajesh said, his voice soft but content. "This is why we work all year long, right?"

Ankit, standing next to him, nodded. "This is what it's all about. Nothing else matters right now."

CHAPTER 9

Reflection and Regret

Determined to salvage their trip, the group spent the day relaxing at the Varca beach, visiting the narrow Goan lanes on rented scooter, indulging in local dishes at beachside shacks. The freshly grilled seafood mingled with the salty breeze offered a brief escape from their inner turmoil.

Rajesh, still visibly shaken by the previous night's events, grabbed a bottle of rum from the counter and poured each of them a generous shot. "To the end of the madness," he said, raising his glass. "One last drink, and we swear to never let it get out of hand again."

Ankit and Sandeep clinked their glasses together, their faces still drawn but willing to let the alcohol wash away the last traces of their anxiety. Amit hesitated for a moment, his thoughts flickering back to the chaos they had just survived. But he too lifted his glass and took the shot.

The liquor hit his system quickly, dulling the sharp edges of his thoughts, and for a moment, he felt the familiar buzz of freedom—the kind that alcohol always seemed to bring. He leaned back into the couch and closed his eyes, letting the warmth of the rum spread through him.

"I still can't believe we were that stupid last night," Sandeep said, his voice slightly slurred. "I mean, we were caught by the police and those goons. What the hell were we thinking?"

Rajesh let out a low laugh, rubbing his temples. "We were thinking we were invincible, Sandeep. We thought we could do anything and get away with it."

Ankit, staring at the empty bottle of rum, spoke up, his words tinged with regret but also a hint of something else. "Maybe we're done with all this... or maybe just one more time? What if we could have a real, controlled good time? We could just—"

"Just what?" Amit shot him a sharp look. "You're not serious, are you? We've already been to the edge, and it nearly destroyed us."

But the alcohol was beginning to dull their judgment, and as the minutes ticked by, a dangerous thought began to form. It was as if the wild, reckless energy from last night was seeping back into their veins. The excitement was still there, simmering just beneath the surface, refusing to be ignored.

"We should just let it go," Rajesh said, his eyes narrowing in thought. "We can have fun without crossing lines. We could bring someone here—an escort, but this time, no wild surprises. Just a night of pure, unadulterated fun without the craziness."

The words hung in the air for a long moment, and for a moment, the group was quiet, as though weighing the risk against the reward.

Ankit, his mind clouded by the liquor, leaned forward. "I know someone. Who mentioned about an escort from Kolkata. He said she's beautiful, smart, and knows how to play it cool. No drama. No police. Just... good times."

The others exchanged wary glances. It had only been hours since the disastrous events of the previous night. Could they really go back to this? Would they fall into the same trap again?

But Rajesh, who had always been the one to push boundaries, was the first to speak. "Let's do it. We can book her for four nights. We can make this fun, but this time we keep it under control. No more chaos. No more goons or police or broken promises."

Amit's head was spinning. It was as though they were walking a fine line between reflection and regret and the temptation of old habits. "I don't know..." he started to say, but the words faltered as the alcohol loosened his resolve. "Maybe one last time. But that's it. No more. After this, we walk away for good."

Sandeep, still unsure but caught up in the momentum, added, "I don't want any more drama.

But... it could be fun, right? Just four days, a good time. Nothing too crazy."

Amit looked at his friends, their faces flushed with excitement. "Fine," he said finally. "But we keep it simple. No more problems. Just a good time."

The Deal with Ananya

Within minutes, Ankit was on his phone, asking for her contact details. He quickly found her profile, a striking woman from Kolkata named Ananya, known for her poise, charm, and an ability to maintain discretion. After a few exchanges, a deal was struck. She would fly down to Goa the next day, and they agreed on a price of ₹50,000 for four nights with all four men—an amount that seemed a small price to pay for the temptation they couldn't resist.

The deal was done. Ananya would be their last indulgence—four nights of fantasy, four nights of escape, before they could wash their hands clean of this chaotic chapter in their lives.

As they confirmed the booking, a sense of uneasy excitement swept over the group. They had learned nothing from the previous night's disaster, but this time, they promised themselves, they would be in control. This time, it would be different.

Amit leaned back against the couch, a strange feeling of foreboding mixed with anticipation bubbling up inside him. The liquor made everything feel lighter, as if they were floating above the mistakes of the past. But somewhere deep down, a small voice of doubt whispered, telling him that they were about to make the same mistake again.

But it was too late to turn back now.

As the final confirmation came through on Ankit's phone, the four men clinked their glasses together in a toast.

"To one last wild ride," Rajesh said, a devilish grin spreading across his face.

And as the glasses met, the echoes of their past decisions followed them into the future. They had convinced themselves this was the last time. But somewhere deep inside, they all knew the truth: men would be men, and some mistakes, it seemed, were bound to be repeated.

CHAPTER 10

Ananya's Arrival

The day Ananya arrived in Goa, the air seemed charged with odd sense of anticipation. The villa, nestled quietly amid the coconut palms, stood eerily quiet, almost as if holding its breath. For a brief moment, they allowed themselves to look forward to what was supposed to be the "last hurrah." A chance to indulge without the chaos, or so they thought, yet, Ananya's presence would change everything.

Amit, Rajesh, Ankit, and Sandeep stood near the entrance of the villa, fidgeting with their clothes. They had made sure the place was spotless, even going so far as to change the sheets and tidy the area. They had agreed, no more mess, no more drama. This time, it would be different. This time, it would be fun.

When the doorbell rang, it sent a ripple of excitement through the group. Ankit rushed to open it, and standing there in the doorway was Ananya—a vision that seemed to step straight out of a dream.

Unmatched Beauty

Ananya stood there, her posture graceful and poised, a gentle smile gracing her lips. The sunlight filtered through the villa's windows, casting a soft halo around her as if the world itself had adjusted to her presence. She was tall, with an elegant frame that seemed to move with a fluidity that made her seem almost ethereal. Her dark, almond-shaped eyes glimmered with an unreadable emotion, as if she had seen more of the world than she let on, yet carried herself with an openness that suggested she was ready to embrace everything new.

Her skin was a smooth, warm caramel tone, glowing softly in the afternoon light. Her hair, a rich shade of dark brown, cascaded in gentle waves down her back, and as she moved, it seemed to sway with a life of its own. She was wearing a simple white sundress that hugged her figure just enough to accentuate her curves, but the overall look was one of effortless grace—unconcerned with the kind of attention she was sure to attract.

Over Friendly Nature

"Hello, everyone," Ananya greeted them with a voice that carried a blend of warmth and melody, like music on a warm breeze. It wasn't too loud or too soft; it was just perfect. Her gaze swept over each of the four men, and there was no hesitation in her demeanor. She wasn't a stranger—she felt like someone they had known for years, even though this was the first time they'd ever met her.

She stepped inside without waiting for an invitation, her movements fluid and confident. It felt as though she had been part of the group all along. She didn't appear to be nervous or unsure in the least; instead, she seemed to fit in effortlessly.

"Rajesh, Ankit, Sandeep, and Amit, right?" She asked, already familiar with their names. There was a glint of mischief in her smile, one that made her seem both mysterious and completely approachable. It was like she already knew them better than they knew themselves.

Others blinked, impressed by her accuracy. Rajesh recovered first, grinning, "Spot on! And welcome to Goa."

Ananya's smile widened. "Thank you, darling. I've heard so much about all of you. And I'm so glad to finally meet you all. Goa is beautiful, isn't it? I already feel at home."

Her words were simple, but they had an effect. The men, who had been quiet and unsure moments before, found themselves suddenly at ease. The awkwardness, which had gripped them when they first spoke about bringing her here, was gone. She had a way of making every room feel less like a collection of strangers and more like a gathering of old friends.

She didn't rush them. There was no urgency in her manner. Instead, she took the time to look each of them in the eye, offering a kind and understanding glance that said, without words, "I'm here to make you comfortable, to help you relax."

Making Everyone Feel Comfortable

As Ananya settled in, she immediately began to make her presence known in the most subtle of ways. She engaged with everyone, but not in the way that was often expected from someone in her profession. She didn't make them feel as though she was here to please them—instead, she made them feel as though she was genuinely interested in them as people. She asked about their lives in Kanpur, their work, their families, their ambitions. She listened intently, her eyes never wavering, as if she was absorbing every detail of their words.

"Tell me more about Kanpur," she asked Rajesh, leaning in with a warm smile. "It sounds like such an interesting place. And I hear the food is amazing. What's your favorite dish?"

For Rajesh the question was simple, but Ananya's genuine curiosity made him feel as though he was talking to an old friend—someone he'd known for years, rather than a stranger.

"It's a city of contrasts," Rajesh said, smiling. "We've got the old traditions mixed with the modern hustle. The food is incredible, though. If you ever visit, you have to try the tunday kebabs."

Ananya laughed softly, nodding as if she had heard all of it before. "Oh, I've heard of them! I'll have to try them next time I'm in town. You all must know the best places."

Her laughter was like a melody, light and free, and it made everyone feel as though they were sharing a private joke. There was no effort, no forced camaraderie—Ananya was simply **there,** and it made the others feel instantly at ease.

Her Ability to Make Strangers Feel Like Old Friends

As Ananya interacted with them, her warmth seemed to flow effortlessly. She made everyone feel important. Even a complete stranger could sense that, with Ananya, they could let their guard down and feel completely comfortable.

When Sandeep spoke about his recent promotion at work, Ananya didn't just listen, she responded with empathy, praising his hard work. "That's incredible, Sandeep," she said, her voice warm. "You should be so proud. It's not easy to get ahead, especially in the world we live in today."

Her words, so simple and yet so genuine, made Sandeep's shoulders relax. When Ankit talked about his family she listened intently, her eyes never leaving his. Even Amit, shared some stories he guarded for years.

"You're good at this, you know?" Ankit said with a grin.

Ananya winked at him, her smile playful. "I like to think I am. But it's all about making people feel comfortable, right? You just have to show them that they matter."

A New Dynamic

As the evening wore on, Ananya's presence seemed to completely transform the dynamic of the group.

But as the night progressed and Ananya settled into the group, the men couldn't help but wonder—what was it about her? Was it simply her beauty, or was there something more? Could they really keep things under control, or would this new chapter lead them into even deeper waters?

For now, though, they were content. Ananya was here, and the uncertainty of the past few days seemed to melt away in her presence.

For the first time since arriving in Goa, the group of friends felt as though they were in the right place, with the right people.

CHAPTER 11

Four Days of Bliss

Today in Goa felt like a breath of fresh air— a far cry from the chaos and clutter of the city they had left behind. The group of four friends, still processing the madness of their recent past, had found an unexpected calm in the warm sun, salty air, and Ananya's lively presence. It wasn't just a getaway; it was an escape, a chance to step into a world where no one knew their names, and they were free to be whoever they wanted to be.

Ananya, with her charm, natural elegance, and relaxed demeanor, quickly became the center of their world. She had an uncanny ability to make each of them feel special, to make them feel like the most important person in the room, even in a crowded, bustling place like Goa.

Day 1: Fun at the Beach

The first day was all about the beach. Calangute Beach, to be specific, with its golden sands, clear water, and vibrant atmosphere. The scooters Amit had insisted on renting parked near the entrance, as the group trudged to the beach. Ananya led them all into the water, laughing as she splashed waves at them, coaxing them to join her in a playful water fight. It was a familiar scene—friends enjoying each other's company—but there was something undeniably different about this time. There was an ease to the atmosphere that had been lacking back in Kanpur.

Rajesh was the first to dip his toes into the ocean, hesitating just long enough for Ananya to splash water on him. "You're not getting away that easily," she teased. He laughed and waded into the waves with the others following suit. The sun was warm, the water cool, and the sound of the waves crashing against the shore made it all feel perfect. Ananya's laughter was like a melody in the midst of it all, and the men couldn't help but smile every time they saw her radiant, carefree spirit.

Ankit spluttering after a sneak attack was also drawn into the fun. The light-heartedness of the day seemed to bring out a side of him that the others didn't often see. He playfully challenged Ananya to a race in the water, something that would have been out of character for him only a few days ago.

Ananya's presence seemed to have that effect on all of them, loosening their worries and inviting them to be a little younger, a little more carefree. The moments at the beach weren't just about the water; they were about letting go of responsibilities and enjoying the simplicity of a perfect day.

At night, over beers and Goan curry, Ananya suggested that over four nights, one of the boys will stay with her, while the others explored the beaches and nightlife, returning only when called back.

"Wait, is this some test or something?" Rajesh asked, half-jokingly.

"Relax, it will be fun. You won't regret it."

She wrote the names on the chit, picked one at random, all of them eager to hear their name.

Ananya shouted: Amit...!!!

For Amit, it was like as if he had been promoted, his desperation was very clear when he shouted: Yes...

Rajesh smirked, "Looks like someone hit the jackpot."

As agreed, rest of them left the villa, and Ananya went in to get changed for the night.

The dim light of the chandelier cast a soft, golden glow over the room as Ananya adjusted the straps of her lace lingerie. It was a delicate black piece that clung to her curves, teasingly translucent in all the right places. She exuded confidence, but there was a softness in her eyes as she met Amit's gaze.

He stood near the window. The city skyline glittered behind him, but his focus was entirely on her. Ananya walked toward him, her bare feet sinking into the plush carpet, each step deliberate and unhurried. Her presence commanded attention, yet her smile held a warmth that made his chest tighten.

"You seem a little tense," she teased, her voice low and inviting.

Amit chuckled, his hand reaching up to rub the back of his neck. "You have that effect on me."

She tilted her head, her dark hair cascading over one shoulder, and closed the distance between them. Her fingers found the buttons of his shirt, sliding them open one by one with practiced ease. Beneath her touch, his skin felt warm, his heartbeat steady but strong.

"You work too much," she murmured, slipping the shirt off his shoulders. "Let me help you forget the world for a while."

Amit caught her hand as she moved to step away, his grip firm but gentle. He pulled her closer, their bodies just inches apart. "What if I don't want to forget anything about tonight?" he asked, his voice deep and slightly rough.

Her breath hitched at his words, and she smiled, a flicker of vulnerability flashing across her face. "Then I'll make sure it's worth remembering."

Their lips met tentatively at first, a brush of warmth that quickly deepened. Amit's hands found her waist, his fingers trailing over the intricate lace before settling on the bare skin of her back. She shivered under his touch, leaning into him as her own hands explored the planes of his chest, tracing the contours of his muscles.

The air grew thick with heat as the kiss intensified. Amit backed toward the bed, drawing her with him until they tumbled onto the soft covers. Their movements became slower, more deliberate, each touch and caress charged with anticipation.

"You're full of surprises," he murmured against her lips, his hands roaming her back, mapping every curve.

"So are you," she whispered, her voice breathless but steady. "And I can't wait to discover them all."

The room pulsed with an unspoken tension as Ananya's lips brushed against Amit's once more. Their kiss deepened, slow and deliberate, as if they were savoring the moment.

Amit's hands explored her back, the lace of her lingerie both a barrier and a temptation. He could feel the heat of her skin beneath it, his fingers sliding along the delicate straps before dipping to her waist. He drew her closer, their bodies pressing together, every point of contact sending a spark through them both.

Ananya leaned back slightly, her dark hair cascading down as she looked into his eyes, her gaze both playful and intense. Her fingers found the waistband of his trousers, deftly unfastening the button and sliding the zipper down. Amit kicked them off in a smooth motion, now dressed in nothing but his boxers. The vulnerability between them only seemed to heighten the intimacy.

"You're beautiful," Amit murmured, his voice husky as he took her in.

She smiled softly, her cheeks tinged with warmth. "I think you're biased," she replied, but the way her fingers lingered on his face told a different story.

With deliberate slowness, Ananya shifted, sliding the straps of her lingerie off her shoulders. The fabric pooled at her waist, revealing her bare skin beneath the soft light. Amit's breath caught as he reached for her, his hands tender as they cupped her face, drawing her in for another kiss. This time, it was hungrier, a melding of passion and longing.

They moved together, their bodies instinctively finding a rhythm as they shed the last layers between them. The heat of their skin pressed together; the barrier of clothing replaced by the warmth of flesh. Amit rolled her gently onto her back, his weight balanced above her, his lips trailing from her mouth to her neck, then lower, each kiss igniting a fire that built steadily between them.

Ananya arched beneath him, her hands roaming his back, her nails grazing lightly against his skin. Her breath hitched as he explored her body with a mix of tenderness and urgency. Every touch, every caress, felt like a wordless declaration, a conversation spoken through their connection.

As they reached the crescendo, their hands found each other, fingers intertwining. Ananya's gaze locked with Amit's, her expression soft yet intense. The vulnerability in her eyes mirrored his own, and in that moment, it wasn't just physical—it was deeply personal, as though they'd let down invisible walls and found something sacred between them.

When the moment passed, their bodies still entwined, neither spoke for a long while. Amit traced lazy patterns on her bare shoulder with his fingertips, while Ananya rested her head against his chest, listening to the steady rhythm of his heartbeat.

"I didn't expect this," he said quietly, his voice carrying a mix of wonder and contentment.

"Neither did I," Ananya admitted, her voice barely above a whisper. "But I'm glad it happened."

In the warm glow of the aftermath, they lay together, their connection no longer bound by circumstance but by something that felt far more genuine.

When Amit woke up the next morning, the sun rays streaming through the curtains, he found Ananya already awake, with a cup of coffee in her hand.

"Good morning," she said with a faint smile.

"Morning," he smiled back. He studies her for a moment, there was a sadness behind her eyes that hadn't been last night.

"Hey, are you okay?"

She hesitated, and gave a look that was defensive and teasing," Don't go all therapist on me now. Last night was fun, let's not ruin it with heavy stuff, okay?"

Amit couldn't shake the feeling there was more to her than she was letting on.

Day 2: Exploration and New Experiences

The second day was dedicated to exploring Goa beyond its famous beaches. Ananya, with her deep knowledge of the area, suggested they visit the Basilica of Bom Jesus and Se Cathedral. The group was fascinated by the architecture, the history that seemed to be etched into the walls, and the sense of serenity that came with being surrounded by such beauty. The stillness of the churches contrasted with the liveliness of the beaches, but it was a kind of peace that they had all come to appreciate.

As they wandered through the streets of Panaji, Ananya seamlessly guided them to local markets and quaint cafés, stopping to sample fresh fruits and local delicacies. She made them feel as though every stop, every conversation, and every shared meal was part of an adventure, and in a way, it was.

At a bustling café by the water, Ananya encouraged everyone to try Goan fish curry. It was something Amit had been reluctant to taste, but Ananya's infectious enthusiasm convinced him to give it a shot. He was pleasantly surprised by the burst of flavors, and soon everyone was enjoying the rich, spicy dishes with the kind of joy that only comes from experiencing something new together.

Ananya's ability to make them feel at ease continued to shine through. Even when they were surrounded by strangers, she made the men feel like they were the center of the universe. Amit, however, noticed how her attention shifted naturally between the group, never lingering on him for too long. A flicker of jealousy pulled him as he watched her laugh with Rajesh, her eyes sparkling. Tonight, she picked Ankit, just like yesterday other's left and she went in to get ready.

The soft glow of the room enveloped them, a cocoon of warmth and flickering shadows. Outside the floor-to-ceiling windows, the city lights glittered like stars, but neither Ananya nor Ankit noticed. All their focus was on each other—the unspoken tension, the magnetic pull that had been building ever since he stepped into the room.

Ananya stood before him, her crimson gown a vivid contrast to her smooth, honey-toned skin. The slit of the dress fell open slightly as she shifted her weight, revealing the curve of her thigh, an invitation wrapped in elegance. Ankit, now shirtless, stepped closer, his gaze locked on hers, every step deliberate, as though afraid to break the spell they had created between them.

"You're breathtaking," he murmured, his voice thick with emotion, the words hanging in the air like a confession.

Ananya tilted her head, a teasing smile curving her lips, though her eyes betrayed a flicker of vulnerability. "Words," she whispered, stepping forward, closing the distance between them until their bodies were almost touching. "They're easy to say. Show me."

Ankit didn't need further encouragement. His hands rose to her face, his thumbs brushing against her cheekbones as he leaned in. Their lips met, soft and exploratory at first, but quickly deepened into something more consuming. His hands trailed down her arms, then settled at her waist, pulling her closer until their bodies melted together, heat radiating from every point of contact.

Ananya's fingers slipped into his hair, her touch gentle yet commanding as she tilted his head slightly, deepening the kiss. Her heart raced, a rhythm she felt mirrored in his chest. As their breaths mingled, she could feel the intensity of his desire, not just for her body but for her presence, her essence.

Ankit's hands found the zipper of her gown, and with a deliberate slowness, he drew it down. The fabric slid off her shoulders, pooling at her feet like a ripple of liquid fire. She stood before him in a lacy red slip, delicate and enticing, hugging her curves in a way that made Ankit exhale sharply.

"You're perfect," he whispered, his voice barely audible as he drank in the sight of her.

Ananya took a step closer, her hands reaching for his belt. Her fingers brushed against his abdomen, and she felt the muscles tense beneath her touch. She worked with deliberate slowness, savoring the way his breath hitched as she undid the buckle and let his trousers fall. He stood before her, vulnerable yet unguarded, his eyes searching hers for permission—for something deeper than the physical.

She gave it with a kiss, her lips soft and inviting, her touch speaking the words she didn't need to say. Their movements became more urgent as they tumbled onto the bed, their bodies tangling together amidst the soft sheets. Ankit hovered over her, his hands roaming her body with a mix of reverence and hunger, as if he were memorizing every curve, every inch of her skin.

Each touch, each kiss, felt electric, their passion building like a symphony. Ankit pressed his lips to the hollow of her neck, his breath warm against her skin, his movements tender yet possessive.

"You feel like a dream," he murmured against her shoulder, his voice raw and unguarded.

Her fingers tangled in his hair, pulling him back up so their eyes met. "Then don't wake up," she whispered before capturing his lips again.

Time seemed to blur as they moved together, a seamless blend of passion and tenderness. Every kiss, every caress, felt deliberate—like they were pouring unspoken emotions into each touch. The tension between them finally gave way to a release that left them both breathless, their bodies entwined, their hearts racing in unison.

As the night progressed, they lay tangled in the sheets, the cool air of the room brushing against their heated skin. Ankit reached out, his fingers tracing lazy patterns along her arm, his expression soft, almost awestruck.

"You're more than I expected," he said quietly, his voice heavy with meaning.

Ananya smiled, her eyes half-lidded as she rested her head on his chest, listening to the steady rhythm of his heartbeat. "Maybe you should stop expecting and just feel," she replied, her tone playful but laced with a hint of sincerity.

Ankit kissed the top of her head, his arms tightening around her. For the first time in a long time, the silence felt full—not with loneliness, but with connection.

And as the city lights continued to glow outside, they lay together, caught in a moment that felt eternal, where the lines between duty and desire faded, leaving only the warmth of their shared intimacy.

Day 3: Lazy Beach Day and Swimming

The third day dawned with the promise of relaxation. The group decided to spend the day at a more secluded beach, far from the crowds and noise. It was a hidden gem, a peaceful stretch of coastline where the sound of the waves crashing against the rocks was the only soundtrack to the day. Here, there were no rushes, no deadlines. Just the sun, the water, and the sand beneath their feet.

Ananya, ever the guide, led them into the water once again. The waves were gentler here, and as the group swam and joked, the men felt the years slip away from their shoulders. Ananya teased Sandeep for being a terrible swimmer. Amit, watching from distance felt a pang of something he couldn't quite claim. Since, Ananya arrived, he haven't felt any unease in his body. Even though he takes medication on time, he hadn't felt lighter and free in ages. It wasn't just the water or the beauty of the place—it was the connection. Ananya seemed to make each moment feel significant, and without even trying, she made the men feel more alive than they had in ages.

The time spent in the water felt like pure freedom. They took turns diving into the sea, racing each other, and just floating on their backs, looking up at the clear blue sky. Ananya's laughter echoed in the background as she teased Sandeep for getting splashed too much by the waves. It was innocent and carefree, and yet it felt deeply freeing.

By midday, they were all lying in the shade, relaxing, enjoying each other's company. Ananya pulled out a deck of cards, and soon the group was engaged in a friendly game, with each of them trying to outwit the others. Her competitive spirit made the game even more enjoyable, and for the first time in a long while, the men found themselves truly enjoying the present.

By night it was Sandeep's turn tonight, so others followed the routine.

Sandeep watched her from the doorway, his breath catching as he took in the sight of her. He had always been a man of restraint, yet something about Ananya's beauty and the way she carried herself made the air thick with tension. The weight of his recent marriage, only six months old, pressed down on him. It was supposed to be the happiest time of his life, but here he was, about to share a moment with someone who wasn't his wife.

"Do you always look this beautiful?" Sandeep's voice was hoarse as he took a step forward.

Ananya smiled, her lips curving with both confidence and a trace of something softer. She turned to face him, the light in her eyes full of quiet allure.

"I do try," she replied, her voice low and warm.

She slowly walked towards him, her steps graceful, her nighty trailing softly behind her. There was an unspoken understanding between them, a mutual acknowledgement of the fragile boundary they were about to cross. As she reached him, she placed her hands lightly on his chest, her fingers brushing against the fabric of his shirt.

Sandeep's breath hitched at the touch, his hands trembling slightly as he reached for the buttons of his shirt. "I—" he hesitated, suddenly aware of the weight of his decision. But Ananya only smiled, her hands guiding his as she undid the final button with effortless ease.

"No need to think too much, Sandeep," she whispered, her lips brushing against his ear. "You're here for a reason."

Her words were both comforting and seductive, and as the last of his clothing fell away, he felt an intense pull toward her, his thoughts clouded by desire. The moment he was fully undressed, Ananya gently tugged him closer, her body pressed against his, sending a shock of heat through him.

She looked up at him with a glint in her eyes, her lips parting just enough to draw his attention. "Relax," she said softly, before leaning in to kiss him.

The kiss was slow at first but soon it deepened into something, as both of them gave in to the inevitable pull of desire. Her hands wandered over his back, his shoulders, pulling him closer as his hands found their way to her soft curves.

Ananya broke away from the kiss, her eyes meeting his, and with a seductive smile, she slid her hands down his chest, guiding him to the bed. She followed him, her movements fluid, as she straddled his lap. Her body glided against his, the softness of her nighty brushing against his skin.

Sandeep's pulse quickened, his mind racing. He couldn't remember the last time he had felt this alive, this full of desire. But even as he responded to her, a flicker of guilt ran through him. He thought of his wife, the woman he had married with such hope and love, the woman who trusted him.

Ananya's fingers traced patterns on his chest, pulling him back into the present moment. "Don't worry," she whispered, sensing the fleeting hesitation in him. "You're here with me now. Nothing else matters."

Sandeep looked at her, his chest tightening, not just with desire but with an inner conflict that gnawed at him. His hands moved to her waist, and he guided her down against him, but the moment their bodies came together, the guilt surged again. His wife's face flashed in his mind—her smile, the promise of a life together, of loyalty.

He pushed the thought aside, wanting to enjoy the moment, to lose himself in the pleasure she offered. But even as he let his body take over, part of his mind lingered, questioning everything.

Ananya sensed the subtle shift in his energy. She paused, looking down at him, her eyes filled with both understanding and something deeper. "You're thinking," she murmured, her voice soft, almost tender.

Sandeep swallowed hard, his hand brushing a lock of hair from her face. "I'm sorry," he said, his voice strained. "It's just... I'm married. I've only been married for six months. I... I don't know if this is right."

Ananya's gaze softened. She moved closer, her lips brushing against his ear. "There's no right or wrong here, Sandeep. It's just us, right now. No one else. No expectations, no promises. Just this."

He closed his eyes, her words sinking in, and for a moment, he let himself give in completely. The guilt didn't go away, but it faded into the background, replaced by the intimacy of the moment. He allowed himself to feel the connection, the passion, and for a fleeting second, it felt like everything was as it should be.

As the night deepened, the act between them became a blur of heat and longing, their bodies moving together in sync, pushing aside the world and the weight of the choices Sandeep had made. But as they finally came to a shuddering, breathless climax, he lay beside her, his chest heavy, the guilt once again creeping back in.

Ananya, sensing the shift, ran her fingers through his hair, her touch soft, almost maternal. "It's okay," she whispered, her voice soothing. "You don't have to carry everything on your own."

Sandeep turned his head, looking at her with a mixture of gratitude and confusion. "I don't know if I'm doing the right thing," he confessed, his voice full of uncertainty.

Ananya smiled softly, her eyes filled with a quiet understanding. "Sometimes, we need to find our own answers."

As he lay there, lost in the embrace of the woman who had just shared something so intimate with him, Sandeep's thoughts returned to his wife, the life they had built. He wondered whether he was betraying her, or if, perhaps, this moment would fade into the past, a memory to tuck away as life continued.

But for now, he let go of the guilt, choosing to stay in the warmth of the room, in the moment that Ananya had so effortlessly created.

Day 4: A Relaxed Afternoon and Growing Bonds

On the fourth day, the group woke up with no particular plans. Ananya suggested they take it slow, enjoying a lazy afternoon at the villa. And so they did—sipping cold drinks by the pool, chatting about their lives back in Kanpur, and sharing personal stories that had never been discussed before. It was a moment of intimacy, not just between Ananya and each individual, but between the group of friends. There was no pressure, no expectations, only a shared understanding that these moments were rare and precious. They decided to go to Agonda Beach

The sun was setting over the golden sands of Agonda Beach, painting the horizon in hues of fiery orange and soothing pink. The salty sea breeze carried the laughter of tourists and the rhythmic crash of waves. Among the crowd, four lifelong friends—Ankit, Amit, Rajesh, and Sandeep—stood animatedly arguing over a pair of sunglasses.

"I swear, this guy thinks we're fools!" Ankit exclaimed, clutching a pair of aviators he'd been eyeing for the past ten minutes. The shopkeeper, a wiry man with a sly smile, shook his head. "These are the best you'll get, sir. Fixed price—₹800."

"Eight hundred? Bhai, we're not here to fund your entire month's rent!" Amit chimed in, his arms crossed as he leaned casually against the shop's bamboo counter.

Rajesh, the self-proclaimed negotiator of the group, took center stage. "Listen, my friend, we're tourists, but not idiots. ₹300, final offer," he said, flashing his trademark grin.

"₹300?!" the shopkeeper barked, feigning shock. "You're killing me!"

Before the haggling could escalate, Ananya walked over. Dressed in a breezy yellow sundress, she was elegance personified, with an air of effortless charm that often left people—including the four men—tongue-tied.

"What's all this drama about?" she asked, her voice a mix of amusement and mock exasperation.

Ankit turned to her, waving the sunglasses. "This crook wants ₹800 for these! Help us out here, Ananya."

She smiled and stepped forward, tilting her head slightly as she addressed the shopkeeper. "Come on, bhaiya. We both know these cost ₹100 to make. My friend here will pay ₹350, and he'll buy coconut water for everyone."

The shopkeeper sighed, his defenses crumbling under her charm. "Okay, okay. ₹350. But next time, no discounts!"

As the men cheered and celebrated the small victory, Ananya shook her head, laughing. "You boys are unbelievable. All this drama for sunglasses?"

Mischief on the Beach

Later that evening, the group headed to a quieter part of the beach, where the moonlight danced on the waves. They spread out a colorful blanket and sat with chilled beers and plates of fried calamari from a nearby shack.

"I have an idea," Sandeep announced suddenly, his eyes twinkling with mischief. "Let's build a sandcastle competition. Losers buy dinner!"

"Sandcastles? What are we, ten?" Rajesh scoffed.

"Scared you'll lose, huh?" Sandeep teased, grabbing a handful of wet sand.

The group quickly split into teams—Ankit and Amit versus Rajesh and Sandeep—while Ananya appointed herself the judge. The competition escalated into chaos as the men argued over techniques, sabotaged each other's castles, and flung sand at one another like kids on a playground.

At one point, Ananya couldn't stop laughing when Amit, trying to steal ideas from the opposing team, tripped and landed face-first into the sand. "Smooth move, Picasso!" she teased, helping him up.

In the end, Ananya declared both teams disqualified for poor craftsmanship and excessive sabotage. "You're all losers, so you're all buying me dinner," she said with a playful smirk.

Playfulness Comes Alive

As evening wore on, they walked along the shore, the cool water lapping at their feet. Ananya found herself at the center of their jokes and playful jabs, but it was clear how much the group cherished her presence.

"You know," Ankit said, kicking at a seashell, "it's been ages since I've felt this free. Like, no deadlines, no stress, just us."

"Yeah," Amit agreed. "Goa has a way of bringing out the kid in you. Or maybe it's Ananya."

"Excuse me?" Ananya said, raising an eyebrow.

"Admit it," Rajesh interjected, "you're the glue holding this circus together. Without you, we'd be four grumpy old men bargaining over sunglasses."

Ananya rolled her eyes but smiled. "Okay, fine. I'll take the credit. But only if you promise to behave tomorrow."

"Not a chance," Sandeep quipped, splashing water at her feet and bolting away before she could retaliate.

As the group burst into laughter, chasing each other along the moonlit beach, it was clear that in this moment, they weren't just four friends and a close companion—they were family, bound by shared memories and unspoken affection.

Ananya continued to make each of them feel special. With Rajesh, she discussed his ambitions for the future, encouraging him to follow his heart and take risks in life. With Ankit, she spoke about his quiet nature, urging him to open up more and embrace the moments of joy that came his way. With Sandeep, she shared stories of her own life, offering him advice and a sense of empathy. And with Amit, she showed an unexpected depth of understanding, talking to him about the importance of balancing work and relaxation, of finding joy in the little things.

For each of the men, the connection was becoming deeper and more meaningful. They began to realize that it wasn't just about the fun or the adventure—it was about something much more personal. With Ananya, they had a chance to reconnect with a side of themselves they had lost along the way, a side that was carefree, joyful, and full of life.

As the day drew to a close, the group sat on the balcony, watching the sunset over the horizon. There was no need for words. The silence spoke volumes, and the bonds that had been forged over the past few days felt stronger than ever. Goa had given them the time to rediscover themselves and each other, and they weren't ready for it to end. Goa had worked its magic yet again, turning a simple trip into a treasure trove of joy, mischief, and moments they'd remember for years to come.

Finally, it was Rajesh night, as other's departed, Amit watched Ananya leave, a flicker of envy crossed his mind. He knew it was irrational, she wasn't his to claim, but she made something inside him tighten. He could only wonder if he had the courage to show her just how much she meant to him.

The room was dimly lit, with the only illumination coming from the soft glow of a bedside lamp. The atmosphere was thick with anticipation, the air charged with the unspoken emotions that had been building for days. Ananya stood by the window, the delicate fabric of her nighty fluttering slightly as she gazed out at the twinkling city below. The satin of her nighty clung to her skin, the deep pink hue accentuating the smooth curves of her body.

For four long days, he had waited for this moment. Four days of anticipation, of imagining what it would be like to finally hold her, to be with her in a way that felt both inevitable and electrifying. His thoughts had been consumed with the idea of this night, his desire for her growing with each passing hour.

Finally, as the door clicked open, Rajesh stepped into the room. His eyes immediately found hers, and for a moment, everything else in the world seemed to fade away. Ananya's gaze was steady, but there was a warmth in her eyes, an unspoken promise that made Rajesh's pulse quicken.

Ananya smiled, a slight curve of her lips that held both confidence and invitation. "You've waited patiently," she said softly, her voice like silk. "Now it's your turn."

Rajesh took a deep breath, his heart racing. "I've waited for this night... for you."

Without another word, he closed the distance between them, his large, steady hands gently cupping her face. The moment their lips met, a spark ignited between them. His kiss was deep and slow, a connection that felt more like a meeting of souls than just a physical act. Ananya responded in kind, her body leaning into him, her hands gliding down his chest as she felt the heat of his body pressing against hers.

Ananya slowly broke the kiss, her eyes flicking down to his shirt. She gave a small, teasing smile before reaching up and undoing the buttons one by one, each movement deliberate, each moment building the tension that had been mounting for days. Rajesh's hands moved to her waist, pulling her closer, feeling the warmth of her body through the thin fabric of her nighty.

As his shirt slipped off his shoulders, he caught sight of her, his breath catching in his throat. She was stunning, a vision of sensuality wrapped in satin. Without hesitation, he reached for the hem of her nighty, lifting it slowly, his fingers grazing her soft skin as he revealed her body inch by inch. When the fabric pooled around her feet, he couldn't help but admire her, his gaze lingering on the curves of her body, the way she moved with a grace that took his breath away.

Rajesh was a man of passion, of intensity. He wasn't one to rush, and tonight, he had all the time in the world. He let his hands roam over her skin, feeling the softness of her curves, the way her body responded to his touch. Ananya's breath hitched as his fingers traced the curve of her neck, down the line of her spine, before resting it on her shoulder. Rajesh's lips trailed down her neck, tasting the warmth of her skin, feeling her pulse quicken beneath his touch.

He stood up, taking her hand and guiding her to the bed. Rajesh's eyes never left hers as he undid the final clasp of her bra, letting the delicate lace fall away, leaving her exposed to him. His hands roamed over her body, worshipping her with the intensity of a man who had waited far too long to touch her, to be with her. He kissed her again, this time more urgently, his passion burning brighter with every second.

Ananya responded eagerly, matching his intensity. Rajesh's hands moved to her hips, guiding her as she ground herself against him, the friction building the tension between them. His lips trailed down to her neck, his breath hot against her skin as he moved lower, his hands gripping her tighter.

As the night wore on, their connection deepened, the passion between them growing until it felt like nothing else mattered. Rajesh's stamina was unmatched, his body strong and unrelenting, each movement filled with a burning desire that seemed to have no end. They moved together, a rhythm that was both sensual and powerful, their bodies coming together again and again as if they were two halves of the same whole.

Rajesh's hands were strong but gentle, exploring every inch of her, his fingers gliding over her skin as if he were memorizing her body.

Hours passed in a blur of heat and intensity, their bodies constantly shifting, never slowing. Rajesh's desire for her seemed boundless, and Ananya met him with equal fervor, their bodies intertwining as they chased a shared release.

When they finally collapsed together, their bodies slick with sweat, hearts racing, Ananya rested her head on his chest, listening to the steady beat of his heart. Rajesh's breathing was heavy, but there was a contentment in it, a satisfaction that only came from truly connecting with someone.

But as he lay there, his thoughts began to wander. He thought of the night, of how he had held nothing back, of the raw passion that had consumed them both. And yet, in the quiet aftermath, there was a fleeting sense of doubt. His heart still ached for something—someone—else.

Was this right? Was this the woman he truly desired, or had his longing been for the moment, for the escape from everything else? His thoughts turned briefly to his life outside this room, to the relationships he had built.

But in the stillness, he allowed himself to push those thoughts aside, choosing to focus on the warmth of Ananya in his arms, the satisfaction of the night, and the way she made him feel alive in a way nothing else had before.

CHAPTER 12

Amit's Momentarily Spark

Amit had always prided himself on being a dedicated husband—a man who loved his wife deeply and was committed to his family. But as the days passed in Goa, something inside him began to shift. There was a spark, a magnetic pull toward Ananya that he couldn't quite ignore. It wasn't just her beauty—though she was undoubtedly stunning—but something more intangible. It was her laughter, her warmth, the way she made him feel seen in a way he hadn't felt in a long time.

Back home in Kanpur, Amit had a routine. His wife, Shweta, was a kind and loving woman, but over the years, the spark that had once defined their relationship seemed to have faded. The small gestures, the late-night conversations, the moments of affection had become rare, replaced by work, responsibilities, and the overwhelming pressure of day-to-day life. There was a certain distance now, an emotional gap that Amit couldn't ignore.

With Ananya, everything felt different. Her presence was magnetic. She wasn't just physically attractive—she exuded an energy that was hard to ignore. Each time they spoke, Amit found himself drawn to her laughter, her ability to make every moment feel special. It was like she brought a sense of vitality back into his life. And as they spent more time together, those small moments—like when Ananya would gently tease him or share a quiet smile—became moments he craved.

One evening, as they sat together at the beach, Ananya beside him, her laughter blending with the sound of the waves, Amit felt an odd sense of longing. He looked at her, and for a brief moment, he found himself thinking about Shweta. He compared the way Ananya made him feel with the routine that had settled over his marriage.

Ananya leaned back, digging her toes in the sand," You are staring and not being subtle about it."

Amit smiled, looking at the waves reaching its shore," To be frank, I have been staring at you since day one."

Ananya chuckled, "Even a kid could notice that. You are terrible at hiding, Amit. You need to stop overthinking. Life is too short for anything."

Ananya smile faltered as she noticed his distant look," Look I get it, it's one of the best days I have had in a while. Let's not ruin it by thinking it is something more."

Her words hit him like a splash of cold water. He looked at her, her magnetic charisma seems to dull a little," I have been meaning to ask, you looked sad the day we were together. Is there something that's bothering you?"

For a moment, her façade cracked. Ananya's finger instantly reached for the hem of the dress. She avoided his gaze, "We are here to escape from reality, Amit. Let's enjoy the day."

He could see she was reluctant to open up, he didn't want to push too hard," Sometimes, it helps to talk thing through."

Ananya left out a soft chuckle, "We carry things we don't talk about. Maybe because we think no one will understand or maybe talking won't fix it. I'm fine, Amit, really."

He didn't press further. They sat in silence for a while, the crashing of waves filling the space between them.

That night, as the group gathered back at the villa, Amit couldn't push aside his thoughts. He walked over to Rajesh, Ankit, and Sandeep, who were sitting on the balcony sipping drinks, their laughter filling the night air.

"Guys, I've got to admit something," Amit said, his voice low. "I don't know if it's just me, but I can't stop thinking about Ananya. There's something about her. I know I'm married, and I love Shweta, but this feeling... It's like she's brought back something that's been missing in my life. The spark that used to be there... I can't help but compare her to Shweta."

The three men paused, exchanging looks, before Rajesh spoke up. "Amit, listen. I get it. Ananya's beautiful. She's charismatic, and she knows how to make you feel special. But this is just a fling. It's not real. It's an escape from our normal lives."

Amit looked down, feeling the weight of Rajesh's words but still unsure. "But it feels real, Rajesh. It feels like there's something more here."

Sandeep leaned in; his expression serious. "Amit, we've all been married for a while. We know what you're feeling, but you've got to remember one thing. There's a difference between a smile and happiness. A smile is fleeting, it's a moment. But true happiness, true fulfillment, comes from a deeper place—something that's built over time, through challenges and growth. Shweta might not always seem exciting, but she's your partner. You've built a life together. Don't throw that away because of a momentary spark."

Ankit nodded in agreement. "We all go through phases. Relationships change, and sometimes they lose that initial excitement. But that doesn't mean it's over. It's about finding new ways to connect, to rediscover each other. Ananya is a distraction, Amit. Nothing more."

Amit felt a heavy knot in his stomach as his friends spoke. Deep down, he knew they were right. Ananya had become a symbol of something he'd been missing, but that didn't mean she was the solution to his problems. What he needed wasn't a temporary escape, but a rekindling of the bond he had with Shweta.

He sat quietly for a while, reflecting on what his friends had said. He thought about his wife—the way she had always supported him on his health issues, the life they had built together. Yes, their relationship wasn't perfect, but it was real. It was built on years of shared experiences, challenges, and love. He couldn't just throw that away for a fleeting moment of excitement with Ananya.

"I get it," Amit finally said, his voice more reflective now. "I've been caught up in the moment, I guess. I just needed someone to make me feel... alive again, I suppose. But you're right. I've got a life back home, a family. Shweta deserves better than that."

Rajesh patted him on the back. "That's the Amit we know. It's easy to get lost in distractions, but it's family that keeps us grounded."

Sandeep added, "And don't forget—what you have with Shweta is real. It's lasting. This... whatever it is with Ananya, it's just a chapter. Nothing more."

Amit nodded, feeling a sense of clarity wash over him. He realized that his attraction to Ananya had been more about an escape than anything else. The life he had with his wife was built on love, trust, and shared history. It was worth fighting for.

He turned to his friends with a smile. "I think I know what I need to do. I'll be friends with Ananya. That's it. Nothing more. I don't want to lose what I have at home."

The other men smiled back, proud of Amit for realizing what truly mattered. They spent the rest of the evening talking about their own marriages, joking about the ups and downs of family life, and reaffirming what they already knew—that family was the foundation of their happiness.

Later, Amit found Ananya scrolling through her phone, her brows furrowing,"Ananya," he began.

Ananya looked up, asking him to continue.

Amit started, "I thought a lot. You are an amazing person, I'm glad I got to know you. I think I need to take a step back, I don't want to cross the limit, even unintentionally."

Ananya smiled knowingly," I understand, Amit. Sometimes we meet people who remind us of things we have lost, but they're not meant to stay. I hope you find what you are looking for."

CHAPTER 13

Emotional Farewell

The final day in Goa arrived, and with it, a bittersweet realization. A week had passed in a blur of sunshine, laughter, and memories—memories that none of them would soon forget. As the sun began to dip below the horizon, casting a golden glow over the villa, the group of friends sat together, silently acknowledging the fact that their time with Ananya was drawing to a close.

It wasn't just the beautiful beaches of Goa or the carefree moments they'd shared that made this trip unforgettable; it was Ananya herself. Her easy-going nature, the way she effortlessly made everyone feel special, and her uncanny ability to make the simplest of moments feel significant had left an indelible mark on all four men.

Over the past few days, they'd grown fond of her—not just for her physical beauty but for the way she could make even the most mundane conversations feel meaningful. Even with all the distractions they'd experienced, it was Ananya's presence that had truly transformed their trip. She breathed life into their bond, reminding them of the joy that comes with being carefree, adventurous, and present in the moment.

They had all talked, laughed, and shared stories with her as if they had known her for years. Her openness made it easy to confide in her, to speak about things they hadn't shared with anyone else. Ananya wasn't just an escort; she was a companion, a friend, and in many ways, a teacher who had helped them rediscover parts of themselves they had forgotten.

Ananya entered the room, her usual brightness radiating, but even she couldn't mask the quiet undercurrent of sadness in the air. She had always been able to read the room, to sense when something was amiss, and today, it was impossible to ignore.

"You guys are making this harder than it needs to be," Ananya said, her voice light, but there was a hint of emotion behind it. "I knew this day was coming, but I didn't think it would be so... hard."

The four friends exchanged glances. Rajesh cleared his throat, his voice betraying the vulnerability he was trying to hide. "It's just... We've all had such a great time, Ananya. You've made this trip unforgettable. It's hard to imagine going back to our normal lives now."

Ankit piped up. "Yeah, you've made us feel young again. We've laughed more in the past few days than we have in years. You've reminded us that we need to live in the moment, to not just get stuck in our routines."

Sandeep smiled, but there was a sadness in his eyes. "I never expected to get this close to anyone on this trip, but with you... it felt different. You weren't just a guest, Ananya. You became a part of the group."

Amit, who had spent so much time reflecting on his feelings over the past few days, finally found the words. "I think what we're all trying to say is... thank you. Thank you for making this trip so memorable, for being who you are, and for reminding us that there's so much more to life than just work and responsibilities. You've made a real impact on us, Ananya."

Ananya's eyes softened as she listened to each of them. She had known, in some way, that this moment was coming, but hearing it from them made it feel more real. She wasn't used to being appreciated like this—especially from men who had come into her life with a specific expectation, only to leave with a newfound respect for her. It was humbling, and in some ways, it made saying goodbye even harder.

"I didn't expect this either," she said, her voice quiet but sincere. "When I came here, I didn't know what to expect from any of you, or even from myself. But... this has been one of the best experiences I've ever had. You all made me feel like more than just an escort. You made me feel like a friend, and I'll never forget that."

There was a brief pause as the group collectively processed her words. Each man was thinking of the time they'd spent together, the connection they'd built, and how quickly four days had passed. It was almost as if time had slowed down just to give them these precious moments—moments that they knew would remain etched in their hearts long after they left Goa.

"Promise me something," Ananya said, her tone playful yet serious. "Promise me you'll keep this energy with you. Don't let it fade once you're back to your regular lives. You all deserve to keep that spark alive."

Rajesh nodded, his usual composure slipping just enough for his sincerity to shine through. "We will, Ananya. We'll carry these memories with us, and we won't forget what you've taught us."

As the evening wore on, the four friends shared a quiet dinner with Ananya, recounting their favorite moments from the trip. They laughed again, remembering the ridiculous things they'd done together—how they had ventured into Goa's wild nightlife, their absurd attempts at bargaining with street vendors, and the way Ananya had encouraged them to let loose, to not take themselves too seriously.

And when the time finally came for Ananya to leave, there were no grand gestures, no dramatic farewells. Just a group of friends who had shared something special and knew that parting was inevitable. Ananya stood up, her suitcase in hand, and smiled at them one last time.

"Goodbye, guys," she said, her voice steady but tinged with a touch of sadness. "I'll always remember this trip. You've all made it unforgettable."

The men stood up to give her a warm hug, each one taking a moment to thank her for the memories they would carry with them forever.

As the taxi pulled away from the villa, the four friends stood in silence, watching Ananya disappear into the night. There was a sense of loss in the air, but also a quiet understanding. They had all come to Goa seeking something—a break, an adventure, a chance to reconnect with their youthful selves. And in doing so, they had found not just a temporary escape, but a reminder of the importance of living fully, embracing the present, and cherishing the relationships that truly mattered.

As they walked back to the villa, the laughter from earlier had faded, but the bond between them had grown stronger. They had shared something unique, something that would always be part of their shared history.

And though the trip had ended, the lessons they had learned—and the memories of Ananya—would remain with them for years to come.

CHAPTER 14

Back to Reality

The flight from Goa to Lucknow was quieter than any of them had expected. The high-energy days of beaches, bars, and new adventures were now behind them, and the reality of returning to their regular lives settled in. As the plane ascended into the cloud-filled sky, the four friends sat together in silence, each lost in their own thoughts.

The trip had been a whirlwind, and as they looked out the airplane windows, they couldn't help but reminisce about their time in Goa. The laughter, the wild nights, the new experiences—all of it felt surreal now, as if it had been a different lifetime. And at the center of all those memories was Ananya. Though they had tried to keep their emotions in check during their time with her, now that she was gone, there was an undeniable sense of emptiness.

Amit, who had spent most of the flight staring out of the window, was the first to break the silence. "I still can't believe it's over. Goa feels like a dream now," he said, his voice distant.

Sandeep nodded, adjusting in his seat. "Yeah, it was a blast. I feel like I need a few more days just to process everything. Ananya... she really did make this trip unforgettable."

Rajesh sighed, a faint smile playing on his lips. "I know. She made everything feel alive again. But we're back now. Life's waiting for us."

Ankit, who had been silent most of the flight, finally spoke up. "Back to work. Back to the grind. The excitement's over."

The conversation shifted to memories of their time with Ananya—how she left a mark in each of them. They spoke fondly of the quiet moments too—the early morning walks along the beach, the dinners they had shared together, the conversations that had seemed so natural and easy. They could almost feel her presence still, like a trace of sunshine lingering in the air.

When the plane touched down in Lucknow, it was like the last remnants of the carefree adventure slipped away. The hum of the engines, the bustle of the airport, the familiar crowds of travelers—all of it was a stark reminder that life had moved on. The four friends collected their bags and made their way out of the terminal, where a car was waiting to take them back to Kanpur.

The drive from Lucknow to Kanpur was long, and as the cityscape blurred past, the men found themselves reflecting on what had transpired over the past few days. Amit leaned back in his seat, his mind still wandering back to Ananya. Was she really as special as they'd all felt, or was it simply the magic of the trip that had made everything seem brighter? He wondered if he would ever feel the same again in his marriage with Shweta, or if the spark he'd felt with Ananya had somehow been the answer to something deeper within him.

Sandeep, in the front seat, seemed deep in thought too. "You know, I keep thinking about how much fun we had, but when we get back to our regular lives, everything feels so... monotonous."

Rajesh chuckled softly. "Monotonous is the right word. Bank work, home, kids, routine. Day in, day out."

Ankit added, "It feels like a reset, doesn't it? Goa was a world of its own. But now that we're back, it's like we've stepped into another version of ourselves."

The car drove on, the sound of the wheels against the road almost hypnotic as the hours passed. Despite the physical distance from Goa, the emotional pull of the trip and the memories seemed to keep the four men bound together. There was no denying that their lives had been changed—at least for a short while.

When they finally reached Kanpur, the men made their way to their homes. The familiar streets and crowded roads were a sharp contrast to the laid-back, sun-drenched vibes of Goa. The bustling market lanes, the honking cars, and the noise of everyday life immediately overwhelmed them. But beyond that, it was the silence of their own homes that struck them hardest. Their families had all been waiting for them—wives, children, relatives—but in those first moments of reunion, the excitement was overshadowed by the quiet reality of returning to their routines.

Amit walked into his house, and Shweta greeted him with a warm smile, her eyes bright with anticipation. She had missed him, and he could see it in the way she embraced him. The kids ran to him, pulling at his clothes, excited to have their father back. But even as he hugged them, something inside him lingered—a sense of longing for the freedom and excitement of the past few days.

Sandeep's wife greeted him at the door with the same warmth, but there was a coolness in her voice as she spoke about the bills, the chores, and everything else that had piled up in his absence. Rajesh, too, was met with the usual questions about work, kids, and household matters. The normalcy of home was comforting in some ways, but it also felt a little suffocating. Ankit hugged his wife, she has taken care of his parents in his presence, and he never felt more grateful.

Days passed, and slowly the men fell back into their routine. They returned to their work, their daily grind of customer meetings, account statements, and the never-ending paperwork. But something had shifted. The hours seemed longer, and the work felt more tedious. The memories of their carefree days on the beach, and the fun of the trip seemed to haunt them in their quiet moments.

Over the next six months, the men continued to live their lives as they always had, but there was a quiet unease in the air. The sparkle of adventure had faded, and the weight of responsibilities was more apparent than ever. They would meet for lunch, sometimes after work, and they would talk about the trip—how they had laughed, how they had felt young again, and how they longed for that feeling once more.

One evening, as they sat at their favorite spot, Rajesh broke the silence. "You know, we really need another trip. This routine is killing me. It's been six months, and I still think about Goa. We deserve to get away again, do something wild, something memorable."

Ankit nodded, glancing around at the others. "I was thinking the same thing. I don't know about you guys, but I feel like I need another adventure. Something that'll remind us we're still alive, you know?"

Amit, who had been deep in thought, finally spoke. "Maybe we should plan something. Maybe not as wild, but something special—just the four of us. We could make new memories, have a new experience. Maybe it's time we get away again."

Sandeep grinned. "I like the sound of that. Let's do it. But this time, let's keep it low key... or at least try."

The four friends shared a look of understanding, the unspoken agreement lingering between them. They had lived through the routine, the monotony, and the responsibilities of family and work. But deep down, they knew they needed to rediscover that spark—that sense of freedom, excitement, and adventure that only moments like the one they had shared in Goa could bring.

The chapter of their lives marked by Ananya, by the wild nights and memories of beaches and sunshine, had passed. But they weren't quite ready to let it go. The world was still full of adventures waiting to be had—and they were determined to seek them out, together.

As the conversation carried on late into the evening, the men all agreed on one thing: they would make another trip. And this time, they knew where they were going.

Bangkok. Thailand. The thought sent a thrill through each of them, and though the details were far from clear, they were already imagining the possibilities.

www.ingramcontent.com/pod-product-compliance
Lightning Source LLC
LaVergne TN
LVHW041850070526
838199LV00045BB/1529